THE VIEW FROM
STEVENSON HOUSE

By Alberta Armer

THE VIEW FROM STEVENSON HOUSE

TROUBLEMAKER

STEVE AND THE GUIDE DOGS

SCREWBALL

The View From
Stevenson House

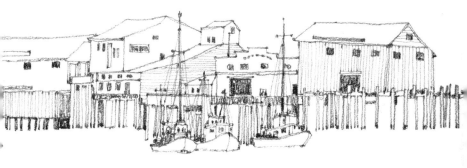

ALBERTA ARMER

For Kitty and Paul
with love
— Alberta Armer

Illustrated by Ethel Gold

THE WORLD PUBLISHING COMPANY

CLEVELAND AND NEW YORK

Published by The World Publishing Company
2231 West 110th Street, Cleveland, Ohio 44102
Published simultaneously in Canada by
Nelson, Foster & Scott Ltd.
Library of Congress catalog card number: 67-23342
Text copyright © 1967 by Alberta Armer
JUL
Illustrations copyright © 1967 by Ethel Gold

For my sister
Anne Roller Issler
who was for five years
curator of Stevenson House

THE VIEW FROM
STEVENSON HOUSE

1

When she had struggled out of the taxi with her suitcase and followed her aunt across the red brick herringbone
sidewalk, Kirsten looked up at the old gray adobe house
beyond the snowball bushes. Square and massive against
the darkening sky, the building revealed dim yellow lights
in all its windows. The downstairs windows were large and
curtainless, and there were two front doors. Through the
glass panels Kirsten could see that one door led directly to
a flight of narrow stairs, the other into a reception room.

The upstairs windows, framed with faded green shutters,
were curtained in lace. The walls of the building ran straight
up to a decorative cornice, with no balconies, no visible roof,
no overhang. A brick walk led past the right corner of the
house, and at the back Kirsten could see a darkened wing.
This was also two stories high, with a narrow ground-floor
porch wreathed in vines. From behind the house came
faintly the sounds of downtown Monterey.

"Why, it's a regular haunting house," said Kirsten.

"A what?" Her aunt's voice was amused.

"A haunting house. When Lorna and I were small we always used to talk about what kind of house we'd like to haunt if we were ghosts."

"This house often does seem haunted," said Aunt Grace. She paid the taxi driver and said, "No, you needn't carry the bag in. It's not heavy." Before he had banged the door and started the motor she added to Kirsten without lowering her voice, "They always expect a big tip if they carry anything for me."

She stooped to unbar the gate and Kirsten, following her, read the large sign posted in the garden:

"Stevenson House
Unit of the Monterey State Historical Monument
Division of Beaches and Parks
Department of Parks and Recreation
Closed Thursdays."

"Do you have to work on Sunday?" she asked.

"Sunday is my big day. I've had as many as five hundred visitors on a summer Sunday."

"How do you know how many?"

Grace Douglas' voice was light with the laughter Kirsten remembered from her aunt's visits in Ohio years ago. "I have a people-counter," she said. "I keep it hidden in my hand or on my desk and click it once for every person who comes through the front door."

"It must be fun being a curator, Aunt Grace."

"I like it." Carrying the suitcase, Grace led the way along the flower-bordered path that skirted the corner of the house. Kirsten saw with surprise that the entire right wall of the main building had no windows. Great patches of plaster had fallen away revealing the brown dirt beneath.

"I live upstairs," said Grace. "Wait here while I set the burglar alarm."

"Burglar alarm!" Kirsten looked back over her shoulder

at the huge dark shrubs and a clump of pampas grass waving its tawny fronds in the damp air.

"Yes. I have to set it every night. We have some valuable things in Stevenson House." Grace opened a door off the porch. Taking a flashlight from her bag, she lit up the inside of the room. Kirsten could see a row of steel filing cabinets along one wall and several ancient rawhide trunks under the windows.

"It's the trunk room," her aunt explained as she adjusted the alarm and locked the door again. "The files are full of historical records and letters. And the trunks have old costumes in them." Grace kept the flashlight lit to guide them through the archway.

Kirsten's spine tingled. She reached out for her aunt's hand and held it as they walked in pitchy blackness through the passage. They came out onto a brick-paved patio, from which Kirsten could see a flight of stairs leading to a narrow second-story porch.

The patio was dominated by a huge iron kettle crowded with geranium plants. "This was once used for rendering whale blubber," said Grace, tapping the round iron side. "It came off a whaling ship—I don't know when. Our gardener, Mr. Tinsley, likes romantic things from far places."

Kirsten scarcely heard her. She was confronted here with another garden bigger than the one in front. A roof-high tree covered with dark leaves and a few large white flowers brushed against the back of the house. The flowers sent forth an overpowering sweetness. Kirsten suddenly imagined herself and Roger there beneath the tree in the California night and her heart ached for his familiar presence.

"Magnolia tree," said Grace. "Right outside your bedroom window. You'll love it. Now up we go."

Kirsten's suitcase bumped the wall, but she kept a tight hold on her aunt's hand as they mounted the steep narrow stairs. Her heart thudded in time to her footsteps, and she dared not look behind her.

"That was Stevenson's bedroom when he lived here,"

11

her aunt said, pointing to a glass-paned door that led off the far end of the porch into the main building. As with the front windows of the museum, the back windows also showed faint lights inside.

Kirsten waited on the narrow porch as her aunt unlocked the door, reached in, and flicked on a switch. A sudden square of golden light flooded over them. The girl gasped with pleasure as she followed her aunt into the room. There were glowing lights, rows of books, and bright pictures between the tall windows. Comfortable old chairs in faded covers stood on either side of a gate-leg table set with blue pottery.

"Wait here, dear, I have one more thing to do before I forget it." Grace disappeared into the kitchen. In a moment the porch and the dark clumps of trees and bushes in the garden below were streaked with light.

"We installed floodlights for the front garden and the back porch," Grace explained, coming back into the room. "I hope they won't bother you."

Kirsten fell with a happy sigh onto the long green couch. "Not half so much as the darkness," she admitted. "I'm an awful coward."

"I know you must be tired after crossing the country on a bus," said Grace. "Come, I'll show you your room." She led the way through the living room into a small hall. "The front room is mine and this is the bath. And this," she added, switching on the light in the back room, "is yours, my dear. Why don't you lie down till I call you to supper? If you want to freshen up in the bathroom use the white towels and wash cloth. Mine are the green."

Kirsten set down her suitcase and looked around the room with delighted eyes. She had stepped inside a sea shell —or a sunrise. Walls, woodwork, shag rug, bedspread all were a delicate shell-pink. Bed, rocker, dresser, and open bookshelves were cream-colored, matching a row of books on the top shelf. Going eagerly to them Kirsten saw that they were a set of Robert Louis Stevenson's works, probably everything he had written.

She carefully turned back the bedspread, grateful that her aunt had remembered how much she loved pink. She tried to close her eyes but she was too tired and too keyed up to relax yet. And too hungry!

In the bathroom she found the light and ran a bowl of warm water. The soap smelled like white lilacs and for a second she wished that smells did not call up associations so vividly. She could see Roger standing beside the white lilac bush saying bitterly, "I had thought of our being married right here in your garden, Kid."

When she went back into the living room she sat down at the gate-leg table where she could watch her aunt in the kitchen.

"I've gotten used to living here alone," said Grace, "and I like it. I practically never go out after dark, so there's nothing to be afraid of."

Kirsten looked up at the door to the porch. Already her aunt had locked it, bolted it, fastened a hook across the frame, and put on a chain lock. She smiled, reflecting that Aunt Grace was not without fear, whatever she said about it.

Grace Douglas divided a small pot roast onto two plates. "Now that you're here we can go places together," she said. "I want to show you all our historical monuments. This whole area teems with early California history. And there's an old theater that puts on melodramas—some very funny things. The audiences cheer the hero and boo the villain. One of our rangers, Max Weidman, quite often acts in them. I think his wife was a professional actress before they married. I should have written you, I don't have a television set."

Kirsten felt too tired to care. "I hardly get a chance to look at ours at home. Six kids, you know, and we all like different shows. Even the baby has her favorites. She likes the commercials." Kirsten looked around the room at all the books. "I see you read a lot."

"I'm hoping you do too. I remember you did when I visited you last. That's four years ago, do you realize that? I don't know what you'll do all summer unless you read."

"I'd planned to copy your favorite recipes, Aunt Grace, and crochet lace for some pillows slips. I guess I've changed since you last saw me."

"Not too much, I hope. I liked you the way you were." Her aunt set down two steaming salad plates, and took her place at the table.

"Artichokes?" asked Kirsten. "I've never had them. They're too expensive in Ohio most of the time. Mama tried them once when she saw a recipe in the *Ladies' Home Journal*, but she said that was too much money just to stick leaves into your mouth and then lay them on a plate." She laughed in some embarrassment. "The bus driver pointed out fields of artichokes as we came past Castroville. Pretty plants. Like coarse ferns."

Kirsten watched her aunt and carefully followed her example. She peeled off each leaf, dipped it into a bowl of melted butter beside her plate, and nibbled at the base of the leaf. She was not sure she would ever learn to like the taste.

"How are they all, your family, Kirsten? You know I've never even seen Hanna."

Kirsten's eyes stung, as for a second she imagined her family around the supper table. Then she remembered the difference in time. It must be ten o'clock in Rockland and everyone would be in bed—except Lorna, who would be watching television. Lorna was sixteen, a year younger than Kirsten, and already the boys phoned her all the time, while Kirsten had only Roger. Lorna was the beauty of the family.

"They're fine, Aunt Grace. Helen's in high school. Jimmy has taken up the violin and he's in the junior orchestra. Hanna is three now, dark like Dad, with little brown curls all over her head, tight curls as if they had been curled on a pencil. She's Arnold's pet. He's so good to her—for a boy, that is."

"Do your parents still belong to the Dickens Club?"

"Oh yes. But I guess I'm the only one of their children who likes to read as much as they do." Kirsten fell silent, remembering Roger's annoyance when she had shown too much interest in her English assignments. He was always so afraid she would be different from the others in their class.

"Don't get all quaint and literary, Kid," he said once. She hated the nickname he had given her. But when she was with him she forgot everything except her pleasure in his company, in the fact that he had singled her out of all the other girls.

Kirsten watched her aunt eat the heart of her artichoke and hesitantly imitated her. She remembered what her father had said, the night before she left. "Try to be a real companion to Grace, Kirsten. She's been lonely for many years. She was so in love with her husband when he died, just three years after their marriage."

"Oh, Dad, why do I have to go? I don't want to spend all summer away from here," then she had added bravely, "from Roger." She was hurt because her father never acknowledged that she was seriously in love with the boy. She did not have the courage to say, "But we want to be married now."

Her father's decision was still her law. "Your mother and I think it's a good opportunity for you, Kirsten. It was so kind of Grace to send you the money for a visit. Not every girl gets a graduation present like that."

Kirsten had been torn between anger at her parents, annoyance at her interfering aunt, and guilt toward Roger, who had begged her to marry him in June. Now June was beginning and she was two thousand miles away from him.

"I'm—engaged, you know, Aunt Grace." She flushed painfully and turned the ring on her finger. The diamond was small, but a real one nevertheless. "Maybe my folks didn't tell you."

"Why don't *you* tell me, Kirsten?"

Kirsten did not lower her eyes from her aunt's serious face. She removed the ring and handed it to Grace.

Finally Grace gave it back saying only, "Very nice." Somehow Kirsten felt that the diamond was smaller than usual. She spoke eagerly. "His father owns a big department store in Cincinnati. Surely you've heard of Jacksons'. He doesn't want Roger to get married."

"You mean he doesn't approve of you?" Her aunt's voice was cold.

"Not any more than my folks approve of Roger," Kirsten answered sharply. "Parents simply don't want you to get married when you're in love, Aunt Grace. They want you to wait till the—the feeling is all worn out and you're able to be—practical and cool."

"What about Roger's military service? Isn't he likely to be called up any time?"

"Well, yes—unless—unless we're married."

"But surely—"

"Certainly not, Aunt Grace. Certainly that's not the reason for his wanting me. How could you think—"

"Then what's your hurry, child? See the world, get some perspective. I know a half-dozen young people in the Peace Corps—"

"We're not in any hurry, Aunt Grace," Kirsten interrupted. "It's simply that we're in love."

"Even so Kirsten, what's to prevent your being in love for a few years while you prepare for your future? In my day—"

"What do you mean, prepare? If we get married we're already *in* the future."

"Oh, my dear Kirsten!" Her aunt carried out the dinner plates, treading heavily as though crushing something underfoot. "Suppose something should happen to him, suppose you had a child to support. How would you make a living?"

"But that's silly, Aunt Grace. What could possibly happen to him?" The room rocked with the silence that followed her words. Kirsten suddenly knew that her uncle's early death had much to do with her aunt's cautious attitude.

She tried for a light note. "We had planned to be married this summer. My friend Em Glade was going to be my bridesmaid if she could lose fifteen pounds. But Dad was against it, and naturally Mama backed him up."

"Naturally. What does Roger Jackson plan to do?"

"Well, of course he'll go into his dad's store." Kirsten spoke with more conviction than she felt. Why should a boy go into his father's store? Why shouldn't he do something he himself was keen about? Was Roger keen about anything?

She pushed back her chair. Her eyes filled with tears and she dabbed at them with her napkin. "Excuse me, I'm—I'm all in, I'm simply dead." She ran from the room. But when she had washed her eyes with cold water she came back shamefacedly and put her arms around her aunt's neck.

"I didn't mean to pry, dear," said Grace. "I'm sure you are old enough to plan your life. I'm worried about your future because—because I know how wrong things can go. I simply want to be sure you know your own mind."

"It's all right, it's all right. I came back to thank you for the beautiful room. You wrote Mama you were doing it over. You remembered how I love pink."

"I remembered, Kirsten. I hope you'll be happy here."

"I'll enjoy reading Stevenson's novels. It will be fun reading what I like again. In high school you have so much required reading you don't have time to browse."

"You really must get to bed now, dear. I know what a cross-country bus trip is like. I'll be at my desk by nine-thirty. I usually work on research for a while before people come. But you'd better sleep in tomorrow, as long as you like. It's very pleasant to have a seventeen-year-old niece here —and such a pretty niece."

"Why, thank you, Aunt Grace."

Kirsten hesitated, wondering if she should kiss her aunt goodnight. She remembered her mother's admonition, "Your aunt isn't sentimental." She decided not to risk a rebuff. At the door of her room she said merely, "Goodnight then," and relaxed when she heard the latch click behind her.

She looked into her mirror and repeated with a doubtful smile, "And such a pretty niece." It was kind of Aunt Grace to say this, but Kirsten knew better than to believe her. She was all too familiar with the slight bump at the bridge of her nose, the too heavy brows and high forehead. She could never find a becoming style for her nondescript brown hair, and she suffered agonies whenever her skin broke out. She touched her jawline, saying bitterly, "Teen-age acne, Mama calls it. Well, I *am* a teen-ager, even though I'm engaged to be married."

She longed for a less boyish figure, for smaller feet, more graceful hands. Her eyes were her only good feature, brown and glowing and set in naturally long lashes. But what was the good of that when every girl she knew could imitate the effect with a make-up kit? "I'm sure lucky Roger fell in love with me."

She opened her suitcase and took out the silver-framed photograph of Roger. Looking eagerly at his intense blue eyes, she longed for them to look back at her. He seemed to be staring bitterly into space, and she could almost hear him saying in his quick, sharp way, "Well, that's life." She ran her finger along the line of the cheek.

Closing her eyes, she remembered her last sight of him. Dad had taken her to the station for the early morning bus, and as she sat on the bench while he bought her ticket, she wondered why Roger had not come for her. Just as the Chicago bus pulled into the station, she heard the screeching stop of the little red M.G. And there was Roger with her sister Lorna. Lorna was laughing extravagantly and calling, "Hey, Sis, wait for us."

Her father's kind face seemed to close up when Roger

18

kissed her goodbye. Kirsten wished she had not seen that sad and angry look.

Then she was on the bus with Lorna's goodbye gift on her lap, and Roger was laughing at something Lorna was saying. Dad made that funny goodbye wave of his, holding up his hand, fingers spread, and shaking it from side to side as if signaling some special message.

Remembering it now, Kirsten was suddenly shaken with sobs.

The bed seemed to be rocking like a bus loping along the highway. Aunt Grace was shaking her shoulder, saying urgently, "Kirsten, wake up, wake up. The burglar alarm just went off and the police are coming."

"Burglar alarm? Police?"

For a moment Kirsten could not separate dreams from reality. Then she remembered. "I didn't hear anything."

"It doesn't ring here. It goes off at the police station downtown when a door is opened in the museum. I have to go down now and go through the rooms with the policemen. I wanted to let you know, in case you woke up while I was gone and heard noises in the main building. I thought you might be frightened."

Kirsten darted to the chair to get her robe and slippers. "I'm going along. I don't want to be left alone here." She followed her aunt.

Two uniformed figures awaited them in the patio. Holding the banister as she went down the narrow steps, Kirsten looked out into the garden. The floodlights channeled through the surrounding dark, casting black shadows behind the trees and shrubs.

"Good evening, Mrs. Douglas. So—the Ghost of Stevenson House walks again."

"Good night, you mean. Hank, this is my niece, Kirsten MacDonald. Kirsten, Hank Borgman and Fred Jones. Fred, I haven't see you since the last time this happened."

They walked through the narrow archway and around to the reception room door. Grace unlocked the door and they all trooped in.

Dominating the reception room, above an old-fashioned music box, was an oil painting of a young man. He was looking directly at Kirsten with amused eyes set wide apart. The lips beneath the slender mustache smiled slightly.

"It's Robert Louis Stevenson," said her aunt. "About the age he was when he lived here in 1879."

The doorways between the square high-ceilinged rooms showed the two-foot thickness of the plastered adobe walls. There was little furniture and the polished wide boards of the floor echoed to their footsteps.

"No use looking long down here," said Hank. He opened the door to a rest room, glanced in briefly and closed it. "If any prowler got in there he came out again. Let's look upstairs."

They went through the narrow front hall, past a combination mirror, umbrella stand, and hat rack. "Grandpa Proudhomme has one of those," exclaimed Kirsten.

Fred Jones, treading on the groaning floor boards above, called out, "This center door's open. Someone's been here since you closed it at five o'clock."

"Someone or something," added Hank. "I insist this may be a ghost."

Kirsten's eyes were round with fright as she joined Fred in the upstairs hall.

21

"That's not funny, Hank," said Grace Douglas.

The big man looked abashed. "No, I really mean it. We were called out this winter to check on a house that the tenants swore was haunted. We never could explain all the things that went on there. People say a poltergeist gets into an old house sometimes—you know, a spook, just to make mischief."

"Well, whoever opened this door must still be in the building," said Grace. "The outside doors were all locked with keys, so he couldn't have gotten out."

Kirsten was looking down the dim narrow hall. "Those bulbs are just bright enough to find your way around the building at night," explained Fred.

"They're so weird," said Kirsten, "like lamps turned low in a story, waiting for someone to come."

"Someone came all right," agreed Fred.

"No one in here." Hank swished his night stick through the clothes hanging around the walls of the sewing room.

"Then he must be in one of these other rooms," said Grace.

Kirsten marveled at her calmness. At each door she unfastened the gate and went in to look around. Curious about the old furniture Kirsten wanted to follow her, but Grace said, "Some other time, Kirsten. Whoever is up here, we don't want him to get away."

On the east side of the hall was a parlor, followed by two bedrooms and, at the end, a children's room full of dolls and toys. On the west side across from the children's room was a sitting room. Kirsten could see a Victorian horsehair sofa with rolled hard-end pillows, and claw feet that seemed to paw at the Chinese matting covering the floor. A stereopticon viewing set lay on a mahogany piecrust table, and the rocking chairs looked almost as though people had just risen and left the room.

"Look," cried Fred, pointing to one of the chairs. "I could swear that chair is rocking." Kirsten's flesh crept.

"You have a good imagination," said Grace.

"There's nothing here a mouse could hide behind," said Hank disgustedly.

They went into the last room—a small square bedroom. A door with a glass pane looked out on the narrow porch to Grace's apartment. "This is the bedroom Stevenson slept in," Kirsten's aunt told her. "He used the outside stairs at night after he had spent a late evening at Jules Simoneau's restaurant." She tried the door. "Locked!"

Two slat-backed chairs stood on a rag rug facing the fire-place. Next to the door was a washstand holding a flowered white washbowl and pitcher, and a sea shell soap dish. But it was at none of these things that all four looked now. Rather they stared in dismay at the bed. Its covers were thrown back as though someone had just gotten up.

Fred flashed his light under the bed and reported what each had secretly feared. "Nothing. No one. Looks as if your ghost was real, Mrs. Douglas. There's no one in the building but us."

Kirsten felt a chill go up and down her spine at her aunt's words, "So the ghost is R.L.S. himself."

Grace led the way downstairs. What had at first seemed a routine investigation, then something of a joke, had turned into a possibility from which they recoiled. They were shaken by the mystery of the burglar alarm, the locked out-side doors, and the unmade bed. Who had slept in that bed? Who could it have been, other than a supernatural being? Reject the possibility as they might, each in his own way could find no other answer.

They went out into the garden, into a heavy and bone-chilling fog. "I should think there would be less incentive to break in if you just turned out all the lights in the museum," said Kirsten.

Her aunt put an arm around her. "I know how you feel, dear. When I first had the job, I used to lie in bed and think of all these rooms dimly lighted as though waiting for some-one. Sometimes I thought I heard boards creaking. And though I told myself that was what happened when wood cooled at night, it was all I could do to keep from getting up and rushing over to investigate. The idea of a lamp in the window to guide someone home always made me feel as though I were expecting Stevenson himself to return."

"And now," said Fred, "it looks as if he has."

In the patio Hank said, "We'll wait till you're in your apartment. And don't worry, we'll unravel this somehow."

"I'd think there was a short in the wiring that made the alarm ring," Fred took off his cap and scratched his head, "but that unmade bed gets me. Well, good night, Mrs. Douglas, Miss MacDonald. Sleep tight." He laughed at his own joke.

Back in the warmth of the well-lighted apartment, Kirsten turned to her aunt. "You don't really think—"

"That it's a ghost? Of course not." Her aunt spoke firmly. "Would you like some cocoa?"

"Yes, I think I would." Kirsten persisted in her own private belief in something supernatural, but aloud she said, "Well, I'm sure a—a ghost couldn't muss up a bed."

"Certainly not." The comforting smell of bubbling chocolate stole out from the kitchen. Her aunt poured milk into the seething cocoa pot and continued, holding up her large spoon for emphasis, "I am sure someone is deliberately sabotaging Stevenson House. Petty thefts have been going on here for some time."

"But why—why should anyone do that?"

"Well, I suppose we're lucky we haven't had vandalism."

Kirsten pushed a marshmallow into the hot liquid, then spooned up the melting bubbly white edges and licked them thoughtfully. "Did you check on that bedroom today?"

"Yes, of course. I always go upstairs before I open up in the morning. At night I lower the blinds in the east rooms so the early morning sun won't rot the lace curtains. They're fine as cobwebs and ready to fall apart. Then in the morning before ten I raise the blinds and look all around each room to be sure it's all right."

"What kinds of things have been stolen?"

"There was an ironstone soap dish in the Stevenson bedroom. Then there was a dresser scarf of hairpin lace. Other things, nothing too valuable so far but they are difficult to replace."

"Possibily different people, not all the same thief."

"I thought so too. But this sleeping in the museum—I don't know what to expect next. You can help me keep an eye out this summer, Kirsten. Maybe your young eyes can help spot the troublemaker."

"Golly." Kirsten had never been asked to play detective before. "Do you suppose someone has a skeleton key to that door in Stevenson's bedroom?"

"Well, I've never heard a sound on the steps at night, but then I wouldn't if I were asleep."

"You said you checked on that bedroom this morning. What about this evening?"

Her aunt, thinking, stirred and stirred her cocoa until the marshmallow was only a thin icing. "No, I didn't go in there at five tonight. I was in a hurry because I wanted to get supper started and get down to the bus station to meet you. There was a family looking at the upstairs rooms just before closing time. They came down a few minutes to five."

The telephone rang.

They looked at each other in consternation. Grace went into the hall to answer it. "Hello . . . What? . . Hank—you did? Just now? We didn't see your light down there. Well"— her tone was grudging—"all right, I guess I'll have to."

She came back into the kitchen. "The burglar alarm went off again in the police station! Hank and Fred came over and just finished looking through the rooms. They didn't want to bother me, but they forgot they haven't a key to the lock on the trunk room door. Now I have to go down and set that darned alarm again."

"I don't see what good it does to set it if it keeps going off and they can't find a burglar."

"Sooner or later they will. Will you come along?"

"Sure. I wouldn't let you go through that black passageway in that big garden all alone."

"Whoever tripped the alarm the first time must be a fool to do it twice in the same night."

"Or awfully clever. He wasn't discovered either time."

Kirsten's teeth began chattering as she stole down the stairs behind her aunt. Try as she would, she could not prevent her eyes from straying past the lighted area among the fog-veiled shrubs. Nor could she believe she did not see wraithlike movements as her gaze went from one clump to another. She followed her aunt through the passage from the patio, then held the flashlight while Grace opened the trunk room door and reset the alarm.

Back in bed at last Kirsten lay staring up at the ceiling, which glowed faintly from the lights on the back porch. She was wide awake. The search through the museum with the two policemen had been exciting, but its aftermath was one of disillusionment and intense sadness.

What a dark musty old place! It breathed an atmosphere of long past days, and Kirsten wanted to live in the present. What was she doing here with a widowed aunt when she wanted to be keeping house in a modern apartment, for a young husband two thousand miles away? What would she do all summer? Even supposing there were young people she might meet, how would she feel toward them? She had never really had a friend except fat Em Glade and then—Roger.

And Roger? What would he be doing?

Tears filled her eyes and ran slowly down her cheeks. When she brushed them away, the diamond on her finger touched her skin reassuringly.

"I've got to stop this," she scolded herself. "And besides there's the mystery to solve. Who really has been sleeping in Stevenson's bedroom?" Wondering, she turned on her side and was soon in a deep sleep.

3

When Kirsten awoke the next morning the room was filled with sunlight. She had a feeling that it was very late. Through her open window she could hear voices in the garden. She leaned toward the magnolia tree. How good not to need screens here!

One large creamy flower bloomed near enough for her to reach out and break it off. She took it with five glossy dark-green leaves that were rusty brown beneath. The flower was like an alabaster bowl filled with lemon fragrance. She knew that it would bloom only one day, then it would slowly turn brown and the petals would fall.

In the kitchen cupboard she found a variety of bowls but nothing that was just right to display the flower's beauty. Finally she decided on a gray pottery pitcher and set it in the center of the gate-leg table. The living room and the kitchen were filled with sunshine filtering through the filmy white curtains. Beyond the garden and across the street she could see a garage yard full of small foreign cars. They were making a great deal of earnest noise, and she thought how Roger would love them. "But they're the only thing around here he *would* like—so far."

She plugged in the coffee percolator and put a piece of bread into the toaster. When she opened the refrigerator she saw against a tall glass of orange juice a card covered with her aunt's dashing script: "Good morning. Come down and see me when you've finished breakfast. Be sure to lock up and bring the keys. They're in the front door."

She looked out into the garden while she sipped the juice. An American flag and beneath it the California bear flag whipped at the top of a tall white pole. Around the base of the pole was a ring of blue lilies of the Nile. A half-dozen young men, with cameras slung from straps around their necks, were coming through the front gate. They wore khaki shorts and shirts and Alpine hats with feather cockades. Two were Japanese, one a very tall Negro, the others blond. All were laughing and one was reading a light meter and unslinging his camera for a picture of the garden.

"Some hiking club, I suppose," thought Kirsten, watching them until they disappeared into the museum.

While her egg was boiling, she collected the postcards she had bought in Chicago and the new ball-point pen Arnold and Jimmie had given her. Then alternately munching toast and egg and staring out the window she wrote a card to Roger:

I had a good trip. Now I am 2,000 miles away and two hours earlier than you. I hope I have a letter today. I miss you so.

Try as she would she could not say more. It was more than the miles. The past few days that she had spent without Roger hung like a black curtain between them.

When she joined her aunt at her desk a little later, Grace said, "You look nice, dear!" But Kirsten knew better. A hot bath had only made her skin blotchy, and fifty strokes of the hairbrush had not made her hair neat and shining. It had that stringy look she detested, hanging around her shoulders as if she could not decide how to put it up. She had chosen the newest dress her mother had made for her, a black and white checked gingham that made her look no more than fourteen.

Kirsten felt that the eyes of the oil portrait above the music box were smiling sarcastically at her. She went hastily into another room, where a family of four was inspecting the Governor Winthrop desk and reading the captions beneath the pictures on the wall. They spoke in low voices.

She followed them into the largest front room, occupied mostly by a huge mahogany table set about with chairs. Bookcases, paintings, and display cabinets lined the walls. Behind this room was a dark parlor whose deep-framed tall windows looked into the back garden. An ancient square piano stood against one wall, and an oak refectory table gleamed with polished silver.

There was a kind of Sunday hush that filled her with awe and a vague discomfort. She went back to join her aunt, smiling when she saw the people-counter concealed behind the top of the desk. Grace clicked it a dozen times as a nun ushered in a brood of schoolgirls, all dressed alike with long black stockings and straw hats with ribbons. The nun paused to register in the guest book lying open in a niche beside the front door.

Kirsten went over and wrote in her large firm hand, "Kirsten MacDonald, Rockland, Ohio." She turned the pages, reading the entries aloud. "Almost every country in the world is represented here, Aunt Grace."

"Lately I had a visitor from Scotland," said her aunt, "a distant cousin of Stevenson himself."

"Oh, what fun," said Kirsten.

"It is except when something goes wrong. Like that night visitor we had. And the stealing. Even though the things are insured it's terrible having family heirlooms taken. Usually people give us gifts outright, but some of these things are just on loan. This morning a silver candle snuffer—"

She was interrupted by the sound of the music box. Grace jumped to her feet and hurried across the room. At her expression, almost of terror, Kirsten felt her flesh crawl.

"But it's locked!" Grace gasped. "It can't start by itself."

She took a key from her pocket, fitted it into the lock, and opened the lid of the long mahogany box. Kirsten followed her aunt and bent over it, feeling at once scared and ecstatic. The brass drum revolved and as the pins hit the tiny metal flaps, the notes of "The Spanish Cavalier" filled the room. All the people in the downstairs rooms gathered around.

The thin, pearly tones of the music reminded Kirsten of grace notes printed in the finest of type. She could still remember early piano lessons and the tiny black dots fluttering among the heavier notes on the pages of her music. But how weird that the music had started of its own accord! It was impossible—ghostly.

Her aunt said nothing until the music had stopped and the people had gone again into the other rooms. Then she relocked the cabinet. "I can't understand it," she said in low, shocked tones. "That never happened before."

Kirsten looked up at the smiling face of R.L.S. in the oil portrait above the box. She could have sworn that the eyes were twinkling.

"There's bound to be some reasonable explanation," said Grace crossly. "Maybe a passing truck started it up."

"I didn't hear a truck."

"I'll ask Mr. Tinsley." She reached into a pigeonhole on her desk. "I forgot to give you your mail. This came at nine."

Kirsten took the postcard with trembling fingers and tried to read it, but the words danced. She wanted to be alone, to make the few sentences last a long time.

Her aunt had turned away to talk to a tall slender man in blue jeans and a blue drill jacket. Kirsten moved over to the window and read as slowly as possible:

Dear Kirsten,
    I guess you're there by now. I sure do miss you, and so

31

does my car. Went swimming last night at our old place. Dad says I'm to start in the mail department. That means getting to Cincy by 8:30 every morning. So you know I'll be getting to bed early at night. I think of you all the time.

Love,
Roger

Oh, so short a message! Now twenty-four hours must pass before she could possibly hear from him again. Turning away from the window, she folded the card and thrust it into the pocket of her dress.

She liked the look of the man her aunt was talking to. The kind blue eyes, set deep in bony round sockets, reminded her of her father's. His tan face was long and slender, the skin drawn tight over the bones, and there were deep smile creases radiating out from his eyes and mouth.

"Kirsten, this is Mr. Tinsley, our gardener."

"Hi." Kirsten's hand was engulfed in a very large one.

"I've been telling him that our music box played of its own accord." Grace laughed, as though embarrassed that he might think her superstitious. "He tells me that he heard a radio report just now of a light earthquake."

"Earthquake!" Kirsten shuddered.

"It was very slight, less than two on the Richter scale," said Mr. Tinsley. "But I think it was enough to start the mechanism of that music box. You know, chickens can feel an earth tremor that people don't feel."

Kirsten chuckled. How did chickens get into this conversation?

"My daughter is looking forward to meeting you," said Mr. Tinsley. "She's down at Big Sur this week; she's a Camp Fire Girls counselor."

Kirsten wished Mr. Tinsley could produce his daughter at once. She was alone here in this old museum with people twice her age and a lot of strangers. Her parents had sent her away from the only boy who had ever cared for her, just when she was discovering how good it was to be loved.

32

Back at home now she would be swimming with Roger, strolling downtown with Em Glade for a dress pattern, getting ready to be married!

When Mr. Tinsley had gone, Grace explained. "His wife's an invalid and has been in bed for years. They have a nurse in the mornings, but when Jane is at home she spends every afternoon during the summer with her mother. In winter she goes right home from school every afternoon. I must say the responsibility is good for her. She's a very nice girl."

"Oh, dear," thought Kirsten, "she sounds dreadful." She remembered the beginning of Wordsworth's "Ode to Duty": "Stern daughter of the voice of God!" Jane would surely be prim, self-righteous, and dull. Bleakly she wondered how she would get through this summer.

"I guess I'll go back up to the apartment," she said. "Tell me what to fix for lunch."

Even lunch, she discovered, was to be uninteresting. "Oh, I always have about the same thing," said Grace. "You can make a fruit salad. Put out some whole-wheat bread and cheese. And then when I come up, you can stir a big spoonful of powdered yeast into a glass of tomato juice for each of us."

"Big deal," thought Kirsten, but did not give voice to her feelings. Her aunt looked after her with a shade of disappointment. It might take a few days for homesickness to wear off.

Kirsten did not have the heart to go down again to the museum that afternoon, though her aunt urged her to explore the rooms she had not seen. "There's a small kitchen downstairs that all the women love, with an old iron range and flatirons and kerosene lamps. And all the upstairs rooms are lovely by daylight. I arranged them myself and I'm proud of them. Even the drawers of the old dressers are filled with beautiful old hand-woven linens and embroidered pieces. Don't let our ghost scare you."

"Oh, I'm not afraid," said Kirsten crossly. "It's just . . ."

33

She did not bother to complete the sentence. She wanted someone her own age to talk to. Roger's postcard burned in her pocket.

She wrote him a long letter, but it was such a futile way of letting him know how she felt. "I must snap out of this," she said to herself. "Now what would Mama do in my place? I suppose she would get a recipe box and copy down Aunt Grace's favorite recipes. Roger's going to expect me to be a decent cook, that's for sure. And if I should have a child in the next year or so, I'll have to know something about sewing. I wish Mama hadn't always been so good at sewing, she really discouraged me. Well, at least I can buy a crochet hook and some thread to make lace for pillow cases."

But instead of shopping for something useful she curled up on her bed and went sound asleep. When she awoke in the soft sunny afternoon her eyes lighted on the row of Stevenson books.

She had not read for sheer enjoyment since her high school senior year had begun. She remembered Roger's comment about Em Glade: "Oh, yes, that literary girl. Is she your friend? But she's fat."

Kirsten read quickly. By five o'clock when her aunt came up, she was well into *The Master of Ballantrae.*

"Oh, Aunt Grace," she cried, "I was going to have supper started. And then I began reading . . ."

Grace looked at the book and smiled indulgently. "Go ahead and read, child, supper's easy to get."

"But no." Kirsten's conscience had sprung wide awake. "Mama said I was always to help you. Besides, what if Roger came home from work and I had been reading all afternoon? Oh, this is terrible."

Her aunt spoke sharply. "It's not terrible at all. You're simply acting like seventeen, that's all—and far too young to be married."

Kirsten wanted to lash back at her aunt with angry words, but she set the table in silence.

The rest of the week went by rather quickly. Every morning and noon Grace would suggest that Kirsten come

34

down to the museum, but each time the girl shook her head. The past had little appeal to her just now, and everything in Stevenson House was old.

There was a daily postcard from Roger. After her first bout of homesickness Kirsten could look forward to the next card and count off the hours like stepping stones across a stream. She made a chart that she kept in her bureau drawer for crossing off each hour. But after a few days she forgot it except at dusk. With each card or letter from Roger she gained more confidence in her ability to "hold" him, even at this distance.

Then there was the pleasure of renewed reading, not just glancing at the morning paper but losing herself for hours. She was grateful to her aunt for the row of Stevenson books. When Dr. Jekyll turned into Mr. Hyde she felt her own flesh grow gross and her nails become curved claws. When Markheim in the clock shop said, "You had better go for the police . . . I have killed your master," Kirsten had suffered with him the pangs of guilt.

One morning as she was taking a postcard down to the mailbox on the front gate, a young man in a stained leather jacket and oil-spotted jeans brought his motorcycle to a stuttering halt at the curb. As she watched him he took off a pair of goggles and stuffed them in his jacket pocket. He was short and broad-shouldered with narrow black eyes that glittered when he saw Kirsten. His wavy black hair was long in back and he wore a heavy beard. Kirsten would have expected him to wear sandals but was relieved to see boots instead.

"Hello," he said, the black eyes crinkling. "Are you Mrs. Douglas' niece?"

"Yes," she answered, and childishly went on in a rush. "I've been here several days. The night I came we went all through the museum looking for a ghost."

"I've heard of that ghost. Come on in, look at things with me. I'm a native son of Monterey, and this is one of my favorite places."

As though drawn by a magnet Kirsten followed him. She

heard him say, "Hi, there, Mrs. Douglas," and saw that he wrote in the guest book, "Manuel Castro, Monterey."

Grace said with a smile, "You don't have to register every time you come here, Manuel."

"Oh, I thought the more people you had the better your chance for a raise."

"Things don't work that way, but thanks all the same."

He knows this place well, thought Kirsten, her eyes following him through the wide door into the next room. Might he be the kind who would break into the Stevenson bedroom at night and sleep there? She decided she had seen too many television shows.

"The Castros are an old Monterey family," said her aunt in a low voice. "Manuel plans to be a history teacher some day."

"I think he looks like a beatnik," said Kirsten. "Or a prophet in the Bible. Why doesn't he dress like a—a human being?"

"He *is* a human being," said her aunt quickly. "He's an individualist. Don't be intolerant."

"We'd call him a nonconformist," Kirsten answered, thinking of Roger.

Fascinated in spite of herself, she followed Manuel and found him bending over the mahogany table, running his finger along the scar. "This was made by Stevenson's coffin," he said.

"Tell me about it."

"He spent his last four years at Vailima in Samoa. He was very happy there with his wife and his stepson. His mother even came out from Scotland.

"The Samoans named him Tusitala; that means 'teller of tales.' But he was more than a storyteller. He was a planter and he hired native men to work for him. He took an active part in politics and wrote a book trying to interest England in the fate of his friend King Mataafa."

Kirsten regarded Manuel with amazement, her dark eyes never turning from his while he talked.

"He was working on *Weir of Hermiston*, dictating to his stepson, when he had a stroke," went on Manuel. "He died the same day. Forty-four years old."

"That's just a few years older than my aunt."

"Now, now, no secrets! His Samoan friends knew he wanted to be buried on the peak of Vaea, overlooking the Pacific Ocean. They laid his coffin on this table, before they carried it through the jungle to the mountain top. That's how the scratch came on it.

"Sixty of them hacked a path straight up the side of the mountain and carried him up on a steamy tropical night."

Grace had come into the room and put her arm around her niece. Kirsten's heart felt curiously open and light as her aunt recited:

"Under the wide and starry sky,
Dig the grave and let me lie.
Glad did I live and gladly die
    And I laid me down with a will.

"This be the verse you grave for me:
'Here he lies where he longed to be;
Home is the sailor, home from sea,
    And the hunter home from the hill.' "

4

Kirsten surprised her aunt next morning by arising when the alarm clock went off at six. She was making her bed when Grace came out of the shower.

"Mind if I shower now and help you make breakfast?"

"Good heavens, Kirsten, of course not."

"I have been getting up awfully late since I came, but I'm getting my sea legs now." She realized that this was an expression Manuel had used yesterday, but her aunt need not know that. Kirsten and Manuel had sat on the bench under the magnolia tree and talked about themselves for an hour.

"Dash ahead, child, I'll start the percolator. How do you want your eggs?"

"I love them boiled and served in their shells the English way—in those silver egg cups you've been putting out every morning."

"Good. I wasn't sure. Your father used to like them that way when he was a boy."

Kirsten enjoyed the stinging needle cold of her shower. She chose her favorite dress, a blue linen trimmed with bands of darker blue. And when she had brushed her long hair she tied a blue ribbon around her head to hold it behind her ears.

Her aunt regarded her approvingly. "You really do look nice. Manuel is a nice boy, isn't he?"

Kirsten dropped a fork and awkwardly picked it up. "He's all right," she said, "for a friend." When she had put out the napkins and popped bread into the toaster she continued. "Do you think it's all right if he shows me Monterey, Aunt Grace? He thought we might walk around to a place called Larkin House this morning. I haven't seen much but Stevenson House."

"Well, of course it's all right," Grace said.

"I mean—my being engaged."

"Oh, really Kirsten!" Grace's voice sounded impatient. She added more gently, "Surely Roger knows that he can trust you. Otherwise how can he love you?"

"Well, exactly." Kirsten felt deeply relieved, especially since her conscience did bother her a little. She had several times yesterday compared Manuel's interest in books and history to Roger's lack of feeling for anything except sports and horses. Not that there was anything wrong with that, she defended him quickly. It was just that she understood Manuel's interests better.

She watched her aunt attack her boiled egg. "Did I tell you about the vicar's egg?" asked Grace. Kirsten smiled to herself. Her aunt had told this story the night before last. There must be a tremendous faculty for forgetfulness tied to getting old. Aunt Grace would be forty soon!

"Go ahead," she said.

"Well, this vicar sometimes served rather old eggs for tea. And when he once asked a guest, 'How is your egg?' the man answered mildly, 'Parts of it, my lord, are excellent.'"

Kirsten chuckled and her aunt said ruefully, "I believe I told you that before. You must stop me when I repeat myself."

"Okay." Kirsten's eyes twinkled. She enjoyed this woman,

who seemed so much more sophisticated than her family back in Ohio.

"Why don't you go down and get the paper, Kirsten?" suggested Aunt Grace out of a companionable silence.

"Good idea."

Shortly before nine the popping of a motorcycle at the curb announced Manuel's arrival. Kirsten had just finished working the crossword puzzle. Looking out of the window, she was surprised to see a young boy on the seat behind Manuel.

Her aunt looked over her shoulder. "That's Louis, his brother."

"Oh, yes, he told me he has a brother just the age of Arnold. Eleven. Manuel and Louis are orphans, did you know that?"

"I've known them both for a long time. Manuel came with his high school English class last fall, and I showed them through the museum. He brought his brother the next Saturday. Louis is almost more of a bookworm than he is. I think Manuel tries to make him old beyond his years. He ought to be playing with boys his own age instead of reading all the time. And I must say he makes himself a regular nuisance around here sometimes. Well, I'm off to work now, dear."

Kirsten watched the Castro brothers come up the walk together. She was disappointed that Manuel was not alone. But when she met them at the door she said, "How nice to meet your brother. Louis, is that right?"

The boy nodded warily. He was barefoot and dressed only in a bib overall. His jutting shoulder blades looked like wings on his thin back.

"Louis wanted to meet you," explained Manuel. "Then he's going down to the beach to play."

"Good." Kirsten blushed. "I mean, how nice to meet you, Louis."

"Hello, Kirsten." When Louis spoke a small dimple fleeted in and out beside his full lips.

"I wonder if you ever read about the Louis Sanchez whom Stevenson was related to," said Kirsten.

Louis looked at her doubtfully. "That man never wrote about any Louis. You're making it up."

"But he did." Kirsten ran to her bedroom and came back with *A Child's Garden of Verses*. "Sit down, let me read it to you."

She knew that she read well and was happily conscious of the serious faces of both brothers while she began the poem, "To My Name-Child."

"Some day soon this rhyming volume, if you learn with proper speed,
Little Louis Sanchez, will be given you to read.
Then shall you discover, that your name was printed down
By the English printers, long before, in London town."

She saw Louis' eyes widen in disbelief. "Louis Sanchez." His own name was Louis Castro, but all three there knew that the Castros and the Sanchezes were kissing cousins. So this poem might just as well have been written to Louis Castro in the first place. Kirsten reached the last verse, smiling as she read:

"And remember in your playing, as the sea-fog rolls to you,
Long ere you could read it, how I told you what to do;
And that while you thought of no one, nearly half the world away,
Someone thought of Louis on the beach of Monterey!"

"Well, what do you know!" said Louis.

"I know this much about it," said Manuel. "Louis Sanchez was the son of Fannie Osbourne's sister, Nellie Van de Grift Sanchez, who was Stevenson's secretary for a while. She married Adolphe Sanchez, a tavern keeper, and Louis was their son."

His little brother was stirring restlessly, twitching aside the white window curtain. "I'm takin' off now," he announced. "Goin' down to the beach, Manuel." He gave Kirsten a quick smile.

"Keep your nose clean," called Manuel. "You've made a conquest," he said when the boy had gone. "And that's something, with Louis. He's got little use for anyone, especially girls. Honestly, Kirsten, I worry about him. He doesn't have anyone for a friend. He's alone most of the time while I work in my uncle's filling station."

"How did you happen to have yesterday and today free?"

"I didn't. I work at night, from four to midnight. Come on, let's get going."

It was one of Monterey's most beautiful mornings. The bay was blue under a bright, clear sky and the houses shone creamy white in the sunlight, making strong black shadows on the brick pavements. Gardens were alive with brilliant flowers, fuchsias and nasturtiums and bougainvillaea.

"Regular tourists get a folder and take a long walk following the red dotted line that runs down the middle of the streets," said Manuel. "It's called the 'Path of History in Monterey Today.' But we'll do it my way, okay?"

"Okay, Manuel. I've seen that dotted line. I wondered what it was for." Kirsten took the hand Manuel held out to her, and they walked along the street swinging their hands.

"This is the Larkin House," said Manuel, going up to the porch where a group of tourists stood about chatting quietly. The curator, a small woman with bright blue eyes and an exceedingly sharp nose, came out the front door with what looked like an armful of flannel underwear.

"Good morning," she said brightly, handing out the stockinets she carried. "Put these on your shoes, everybody. Our rugs are priceless. Hello, Manuel."

"Hi, Miss Rose. This is Kirsten MacDonald, Mrs. Douglas' niece. She's here from Ohio for the summer. Miss Rose Crosby, Kirsten."

"Hello, Kirsten. Grace told me all about you. You're the one's going to be married soon. When?"

"This fall," said Kirsten. She hoped—or did she—that Manuel heard those words.

When she had herded them all into the front room, Miss Rose Crosby raised her voice to a sort of official whine. "Thomas Larkin was the United States Consul to the Mexican Government. He started this house around 1834 and it was finished in three years. Monterey was the first capital of California."

The rooms glowed with the rich and beautiful colors of antique oriental rugs and old silver. Sunlight twinkled on the cut glass and through the prisms in the elaborate tiered chandeliers. The curator's voice went on ahead of them . . . "portrait by Sir Joshua Reynolds . . . Mexican onyx clock made in France . . ." but Kirsten, still holding Manuel's hand, knew she would always especially remember one object—a "memorial picture" embroidered by a girl of ten. On gravestones with mourners kneeling beside them she had worked, in tiny stitches, the names of her dead family.

"Oh, Manuel," she sighed, "imagine that poor kid."

In the garden the curator showed them the house where William Tecumseh Sherman had lived in 1847.

"No doubt you have all heard of the Sherman rose," she said. "While Sherman was staying here he fell in love with a Monterey belle. He told her he would come again before this rosebush bloomed. But he never returned. The girl went into a convent and died of a broken heart."

Manuel pulled Kirsten away from the crowd. "Let's slip off before they ask us to join the retired persons," he said. "I want to show you Colton Hall, where our state constitution was drawn up."

The impressive two-story stone building dominated a rise of velvet lawn in the heart of town. "The first public school was opened on the lower floor in 1849," said Manuel leading her up the outside stairway to the second floor. Inside, in a spacious white room, he showed her where the Constitutional Convention had met. "That was in 1849 too," he said. "Reverend Walter Colton was chairman. He was the first American mayor of Monterey—they called him *alcalde*— means the same thing. Quite a guy. He established the first California newspaper in 1846 and impaneled the first United States jury that same year. Remember this was three years before the Gold Rush. California was actually admitted as a State in 1850."

As Kirsten, like a dutiful schoolgirl, began to read the captions beneath the photographs Manuel tugged at her hand. "Come on. I want to show you the jail."

She followed him outside and to the rear of the building. When she backed away from the small, dark, airless cubicles built into the adobe walls he was sympathetic.

"This will be enough for one morning," he said and seizing her hand began to walk back to Stevenson House. "Kirsten, you're a sport," he said. "I wish you were my sister."

In vexation she dropped his hand. Sister! My goodness, why did she like this boy so much? Why should she want him to say something more romantic? "I must be very fickle," she thought guiltily.

Aloud she said, "Manuel, you could earn money as a guide."

He laughed. "I don't think it would pay as well as servicing people's cars. Kirsten—that *is* an engagement ring you're wearing, isn't it?"

"Yes." She felt at once scolded and relieved. "Oh Manuel, yes, let me tell you about Roger."

5

K irsten was looking into the tiny kitchen on the first floor of the museum one morning when suddenly she heard voices from the reception room. She recognized the pleasant English accents of Mr. Tinsley, and there was also a high, fresh voice with a quality that Kirsten identified, even before she saw Jane, as gay.

"She in here?" said Jane and stood there in the doorway before Kirsten could stir. "Hello, Kirsten, I've heard all about you," she said with engaging friendliness.

Jane wore her blond hair in a smooth sheaf of wheat-gold to her shoulders. Her blue-green eyes were narrow and her temples and cheeks were powdered thickly with light freckles. In her white blouse, short blue-denim skirt, and white patterned stockings, she looked like a model straight out of the pages of *Seventeen*. She carried a summer basket of woven straw with a hinged lid decorated with cherries and daisies.

Jane seized Kirsten's hand and drew her away from her contemplation of stone metates and iron cooking pots. Kirsten was uneasy with this pretty, self-assured girl, so different from her fat, modest chum Em Glade.

"Come on," said Jane, "let's get out of here."

When they had come out the front door, Jane asked, "Did anyone show you the walk made out of whalebones? It's Papa's pride 'n' joy. Look!" She brushed aside the tiny leaves of baby tears that covered the ground near the white picket fence. Kirsten saw rounded knobs like steppingstones in a row. "Backbone of a whale," explained Jane. Then she laughed merrily and seized Kirsten's hand. "And that's all the sight-seeing you'll get out of me. I bet you've been up to your ears in it."

"Well, Aunt Grace promised she'd show me every historical monument in the city. And Manuel Castro has already shown me Larkin House and Colton Hall."

"Oh, Manuel." Kirsten was puzzled by the look Jane gave her. Respect, envy, amusement? "He's too much."

"He sure knows a lot of history."

"And pushes it at you. We graduated together this spring."

They went around to the back garden and sat on the bench beneath the magnolia tree, their feet in a round bed of ivy. Kirsten looked out over the garden. Jane's father had edged a nearby flower bed with driftwood, which curled like smoke, and had set religious shrines among the shrubs. Birdhouses hung from the lower branches of some of the trees, and a single white rose vined over the brick wall by the back gate.

Mr. Tinsley came out of the tool shed hidden at the far side of the museum and began raking the gravel paths, eliminating the morning footsteps. Jane looked across at him and jumped up. "Come on, Kirstie, let's go up to your aunt's apartment where we can talk."

Kirsten's heart warmed to her. No one ever called her Kirstie except her brother Arnold. They mounted the steps to the porch. Kirsten pointed to the door opposite her aunt's.

"Did you know that Robert Louis Stevenson slept in that room?"

"Oh, sure."

Kirsten lowered her voice. "But he slept in it again the other night."

"Oh, come off it, Kirstie. Papa told me about the ghost. You don't really believe that. Like the music box that played by itself, only it turned out to be a small earthquake."

"I'd like to hear a reasonable explanation for that mussed-up bed," snapped Kirsten. She unlocked the door and they went into the living room.

While Jane curled up at the end of the couch, Kirsten went into her bedroom for the silver-framed picture of Roger. She wanted this pretty girl to accept her as an equal not just as a guest.

"My fiancé," she said, returning and presenting the picture.

Jane took the picture and looked a long time at the light blue eyes. "Handsome," she said.

It was not enough. Kirsten wanted her to rave. "He was a popular boy," she said defensively. "Girls, teachers, everyone liked him. His folks were divorced. He—"

"Tell me how you met him."

Kirsten wondered even now how Roger could have fallen in love with her. She was painfully aware of her thin legs and large feet, her uneven locks, the bumps on her skin. She wished she had had a postcard or letter from Roger that morning to reassure her. She spoke slowly.

"His grades were down and he couldn't stay on the team unless he could get C's. He's not dumb," she added hastily, "he just—didn't care much about math and history and English. And I did, so . . ."

"Kirstie to the rescue," chanted Jane, "ta ra—ta ra—ta ra."

"Oh, cut it out." Kirsten was annoyed. "It wasn't like that. He asked me to help him with a problem in class one day and I showed him how—it was so simple. Then he said I had nice eyes. And—"

"I get the picture. One thing led to another—"

"Roger isn't a very happy person," went on Kirsten quietly. "His father and mother were divorced when he was eleven. He hates his dad and still he lives with him and works for him."

"Works for him?"

"His dad has a department store in Cincinnati. Some people say he spoils Roger. He gave him a red M.G. for a graduation present. I think he's afraid of losing him. Roger visits his mother every summer in Saratoga."

"Where all the races are?"

"Yes. She's very sporty."

"And you're not like that at all. Maybe that's why he likes you."

"Well, he did tell me he hates his mother too. She ran away." Kirsten was glad to get this all said. It disturbed her and she needed to put it into words. "So he thinks we can do better than that. He wanted us to get married this June. My folks said no. And I just couldn't do it till they agree."

"I bet that made him mad."

"It did." She spoke proudly. "Half a dozen girls in our class were married while they were in school, and two have babies now. Roger doesn't see what makes me so special." She laughed shakily. "My folks talked me into coming out to visit Aunt Grace for the summer. Dad said it would give me perspective."

"Sounds like a good idea. I wouldn't dream of getting married yet. I want to do a lot of things. I'd like to be a physical therapist, work in a hospital. I suppose because I'm pretty good at taking care of Mama." Jane's voice was quiet but self-assured. "She's had crippling bursitis for years."

"Well, I don't want perspective. I want Roger." Suddenly the tears spilled over and ran down Kirsten's cheeks. "I haven't heard from him in days. Last week he wrote every day." She dabbed at her eyes and Jane, raising the lid of her flowered basket, handed her a handkerchief. Kirsten laughed as she wiped away her tears. "I bet you're the kind of girl who's never without a hankie. I always am."

"Cheer up, Kirstie, if he forgets you you'll get over it."

"That's a horrible thing to say," blazed Kirsten.

"I've been in love dozens of times," answered Jane. "The first time it's bad. After that—pfft!"

"Oh, Jane, I'm talking about real love, enough to make you promise to marry a boy."

"I don't intend to marry a boy," said Jane proudly. "I intend to marry a man. And I'll be a woman, not just a schoolgirl in my middle teens."

"But our grandmothers married at sixteen or so."

"Fiddledeedee, to quote my own grandma," cried Jane. "We're *not* our grandmothers, Kirstie. Life has all kinds of possibilities for us if we just keep free of entanglements for a little while. Otherwise . . ." she paused, tipping her pretty head and staring at Roger's picture ". . . otherwise if you don't do all the fun things that belong to being young you may live to hate the person that ties you down. Like Roger's mom and dad. If you're sure of yourself you can take a lot from someone else."

She lurched to her feet and pulled Kirsten up with her. "Come on, let's walk down Alvarado Street and look at all the fellows in uniform."

"Oh, Jane!" Kirsten tried to draw her hands away, but there was a lightning flicker of interest in her mind. She followed Jane into her bedroom and watched her brush a faint green shadow onto her eyelids, then with a black pencil tilt the outer corners of her blue-green eyes. "Dad doesn't like this so I'll take it off before I go home," Jane said, laughing.

Listlessly Kirsten found a comb and pulled it through her lanky hair. Jane took the comb away from her. "Look, let me fool with your hair." She pulled Kirsten's long hair up in a ponytail to the top of her head. She combed the sides, trying to swirl them into waves.

49

"I hate my hair," complained Kirsten. "That and my so-called 'teen-age skin.' It's just plain acne."

"You'll outlive your skin. Your eyes are what count. And your mouth isn't bad."

"Well, thanks."

"Come on, let's wet your hair a little and maybe we can train it. A London cut would look good with your big eyes."

Kirsten looked doubtful.

"Oh, come on, I cut my mother's hair all the time. I'm good enough to be a barber. Has your aunt got some sharp scissors?"

"I don't know. I'll look."

Caught up in her new friend's swooping efficiency Kirsten led her across the threshold. Her aunt's room was crowded with heavy old mahogany furniture, with a rich red and gold Chinese wall hanging above a chest of drawers. Kirsten began to rummage through the upper drawer. She gave an exclamation that brought Jane to her side.

She was holding a photograph of a gaunt and homely man, with a thin bent nose and thin-lipped sensitive mouth. "Uncle William," she said staring. "I wonder why she doesn't keep it out where she can look at it? I'd want to. Oh, here's her mending basket." Kirsten shoved the picture into the drawer.

Jane carried a pair of glinting scissors back to the other bedroom and, tongue between her teeth, began to cut Kirsten's hair.

"My boy friend would like you, I bet," Jane said presently.

"So you do have a special boy friend."

"Oh, sure. He works in the supermarket right behind the back garden here. He's going to Monterey Peninsula College this fall. He plans to be a doctor some day. Mostly he's nuts about fishing and sea life. His mother and sister are nurses. What are *you* going to do—besides be married?"

Kirsten looked away from the mirror. "I guess I'll just be a wife."

"And buy all the latest products advertised on television.

Honestly, Kirstie, don't you think you should go on alone a little longer? What if you have a child right away? I saw a young couple down in Big Sur, camping near us. Outside of little Jimmie they didn't have a word to say to each other in the two weeks I saw them. How's Roger going to stay out of the army?"

"Well, if we're married this fall . . ." Kirsten spoke before she realized how it sounded. She went on lamely, "I guess he'll take his chance along with Manuel and—what's your friend's name?"

"Harry Andrews. He's kind of a nice fellow, Kirsten, really nice. Now you can look at yourself."

Kirsten hardly recognized her image. The bangs made her eyes look enormous. "Gee, it looks great!"

"You've got a tiny bit of natural wave, but you couldn't get the good of it when it was too long." Jane glanced at a watch on her freckled wrist. "If we hurry we can go to Fisherman's Wharf before lunch. Come on."

The downtown streets were crowded with soldiers from nearby Fort Ord. Cars from every state in the Union flowed down the main highway toward the bay. Old Spanish adobe houses with balconies were wedged among bright modern service stations and drive-in markets. Women elbowed each other in and out of the busy stores. Up a side street Kirsten saw a row of little girls in long white dresses and veils emerging from a church.

She felt a rush of joy and vitality as she and Jane crossed the street and started up Fisherman's Wharf. Morning breezes from across the water had blown away the early fog. Every person was edged with sunlight; their bodies seemed painted on the scene in clean, sharp, bright lines.

Jane stopped to look into a shop window, not at the display of costume jewelry but at the reflection of two sailors. Kirsten had soon realized that they were being followed by the way Jane began to carry her pretty head—as though she were stepping to the end of a diving board.

Everywhere they smelled frying fish and hot grease. A gull soared off the top of a piling, swooped down to the saucer of sand beach, then back to his perch. Two small Japanese children, with shining black hair, rode around and around on a two-horse carrousel.

They passed doorways hung with baskets of sea shells, coral, and seaweed, and tables of crushed ice on which lay huge salmon, halibut, sole, and thorny bocaccio. Jane pointed out squid, crab, shrimp, and scallops displayed behind glass counters.

At the end of the pier they entered a shop where fishing-party boats were for hire. "Hi, Mac," Jane said, "how're they biting?"

A young man looked up from a Batman comic book. "Fair but they're small this year."

"Too bad. Harry wants to try his luck in the fishing derby."

"I heard he was working in the supermarket."

"Only part time. Nothing's gonna interfere with the serious business of fishing—not for Harry."

"Well, they've only averaged seven or eight pounds so far. You and your girl friend wanna go out? Next trip's at one."

"No. Just bumming around this time. We'll see you."

Two sea lions under the wharf began to bark. "Feeding time," said Jane. "Let's get some sardines."

She bought a quarter's worth and they stood among the tourists throwing down pieces of the smelly fish. The older animal, half blind, dived and glided among the piles, then swam out into a clear space and looked up with his good eye at the laughing faces. He begged raucously, caught a sardine with a snap, belched, and barked for more. Jane emptied the bag into the water and both sea lions plunged and gobbled as the girls hurried away.

"We've got time for a shrimp cocktail," said Jane. "You are hungry, aren't you?"

Kirsten giggled. "Since my lunch is mostly tomato juice and powdered yeast I don't think that would spoil my appetite."

As they climbed up on the high stools and wrapped their legs around the rungs, one of the sailors who had continued to follow them came closer and said, "We'll take you to a real lunch, girls."

Without looking at him Jane said rudely, "Get lost!" Kirsten wished she could have done that.

"Watch the tabasco, Kirstie, it's really hot. Have some more oyster crackers?"

"We've got to rush, Jane. Can we make it back in ten minutes?"

"Surest thing you know. Grab a handful of crackers while I pay."

Jumping off her stool and racing up the wharf with Jane, Kirsten thought, "I honestly don't know when I've had such fun."

Suddenly she noticed that her engagement ring was not on her hand. She remembered laying it on the dresser in the morning. She realized too that it had been several days since she had thought to cross off one of the hours that stood between her and reunion with Roger.

6

"Lunch is on the table, Kirsten," said Grace. "I see you got your hair cut. I liked it long." Kirsten knew by her aunt's abrupt manner that she had displeased her.

"I didn't think you'd care how I wear my hair," she said meekly.

"It's *your* hair, after all."

"I didn't think we were late," apologized Kirsten.

"You're not late." Grace nibbled at a piece of cheese and poured out cups of scalding tea, staring down at the pot in her hand.

"Golly, Aunt Grace, what did I do?" asked Kirsten.

Her aunt buttered a small piece of bread before she answered. "I assume the two of you went through my bureau drawers," she said in icy tones.

"You assume . . ." Kirsten let the word hang while she

56

tried to think what her aunt could mean. Then she remembered. "Oh. Yes, we were looking for a pair of scissors to cut my hair." At first she was too annoyed to defend herself, but then she could not help adding, "I've been here almost two weeks and I've never been in your room before. I'm not the least bit nosy."

When her aunt did not answer, Kirsten continued, "We did find a picture in your top drawer, and we looked at it."

Grace was staring out the window. "It was a picture of my husband, I'm sure you knew that. You didn't put it back where you found it. You slid it under the drawer lining. That's how I knew."

Kirsten leaned forward and spoke earnestly. "Aunt Grace, why do you hide him away like that? Such a wonderful face!"

At once her aunt left the room and returned with the picture. She stood it on the table and looked at it as she drank her tea. "I put it away when I knew you were coming out this summer. He wasn't young like Roger nor handsome in any conventional sense. I couldn't bear to think someone so young and carefree might look at William's face and perhaps wonder why I had loved him."

"But I'm not carefree," said Kirsten sadly. "I wish you knew how far from carefree I feel."

"Oh, good heavens, Kirsten!" Her aunt's voice was contrite. "I forgot this." She took a letter from her pocket and gave it to Kirsten.

The girl's hand trembled. "May I be excused?" she said and ran to her room. There, curled up on her bed, she read Roger's letter. It was full of awkward expressions of love, but she did not notice the awkwardness. Only the last line disturbed her, "I go out to your house every evening to hear what your folks have heard from you. They're usually busy but Lorna reads me your letters."

Kirsten stared out the window. "I'll just bet she does," she thought. Then she got her diamond ring from the dresser and put it back on. It made her feel safe and sure of herself, a talisman of Roger's love.

She went to help her aunt clear up the lunch dishes. "Manuel was in this morning," said Grace presently.

"Oh?" Kirsten wished she were not aware of her suddenly quickened heartbeats.

"He's worried about his brother because he's alone so much of the time. Louis reads all those trashy blood-and-thunder books. Can't be good for him. During the day he wanders everywhere alone. He's in and out of Stevenson House so often I swear people must think he belongs here. And he won't keep himself clean, Manuel says."

"Sounds natural to me." Kirsten smiled as she looked out the window and saw Louis entering the front gate. "Sounds a lot like my brother Arnold."

"Louis is a lonely boy, not like your brother with a large family around him. He needs someone. Manuel does too."

"Don't they have any family at all? I thought—"

"There are lots of cousins. When his Aunt Rhetta died his Uncle Pedro married again. He has nothing against the present wife, Maria, but they live out in Castroville and he won't go to live with them. He insists on keeping Louis with him, but he's too young to know how to take care of a small boy."

"*Too young!* Manuel's eighteen."

"I still say too young. In this day and age—"

"Oh Aunt Grace, that's Dad's favorite saying. He always uses it when he's going to make some unpleasant remark about modern youth."

After her aunt had gone back to work, Kirsten ran down the steps into the back garden, where Louis Castro was playing alone. He had a handful of beautiful "aggie" marbles and in the shade of the back gate he threw them on the gravel and "took turns" shooting at them with a white taw. The boy looked up shyly.

"Hi, Kirsten. My brother is comin' back after lunch. He missed you this morning."

She sat on a bench and watched him play in the neatly raked gravel path. After a long impatient wait she decided

Manuel had changed his mind about coming and went back upstairs. Today she really was going to begin copying recipes.

It was past three when the noise of Manuel's motorcycle interrupted her work. She ran down and met him at the front gate.

The fascination of this boy was in his strangeness, she decided—his dark looks, his glittering eyes. She told herself that she hated long hair and beards. She was sure she could not care whether she ever saw him again. It was simply that he was like a hero or a villain in an exciting story.

Manuel's eyes crinkled and he took both her hands. "Say-y, I like your haircut. How much did that set you back?"

"Nothing. Jane Tinsley cut it for me."

"Oh, Jane, eh? She back?"

"You must know she is, you seem to know all about her!" Kirsten spoke with asperity.

"I kinda like to say her name. How's about a hamburger with me somewhere?"

Kirsten smiled and nodded. "Funny, I *am* hungry. My aunt was mad at me and I didn't eat much lunch. But I had a shrimp cocktail with Jane this morning."

Manuel led her to the motorcycle. Without a word she climbed up behind him. He turned then, grinned, and shouted above the popping noise, "Jane never would ride with me. Put your arms around my waist and hang on."

They went slowly up to the end of Houston Street, then turned left and continued across several main thoroughfares until they were on Fremont Avenue. There he put on speed and swept along, popping, among the cars. Kirsten gasped with excitement. The wind caught at her face and whipped her short hair into a tangle. Her arms tightened in fear. With one hand Manuel reached up and shifted her death-clutch from his lungs to his abdomen.

He turned off the highway into a residential street, drove slowly past yards gay with flowers, then turned back onto the highway again. They came finally to a halt outside a drive-in.

"Come on, this is a good place. Let's go inside. Do you like onions?"

"Yes I do."

He guided her to a booth. "Good girl. Jane never eats onions."

Kirsten wondered why she should feel so miserable. She tried to make bright small talk but Manuel was uncomfortably silent. She was twisting the diamond ring on her finger by the time the hamburgers came. They were hot and sizzling, so delicious that she forgot everything except how good hers tasted.

Manuel stopped in the middle of a bite to say, "That was Jane's house we passed on that side street."

Kirsten had difficulty swallowing. "You do like her, don't you? Why did you look me up then?"

"I don't think Jane would give me the time of day. Too much competition."

"And my competition is too far away to threaten you," Kirsten spoke angrily.

He reached a hand across the table and laid it on hers. "Don't be cross, Kirsten, I need a sister to talk to." Her heart melted. "Jane's funny. For a girl who's completely with it, she's got an old-fashioned look somehow, don't you think? Something clean and fresh about her. Her dad's so careful of her you'd think she was made of glass."

"My father's careful about me too," answered Kirsten primly.

Manuel patted her hand. "Of course he is, I can tell that. You're more—quaint almost, for want of a better word."

"Quaint! I like that."

"All I mean is—Oh, skip it. I guess Jane's father knows she's safe with old Harry Andrews."

"Jane says Harry is a nice fellow."

"Oh, sort of. He's so serious about his future. And then that passion of his for anything about the ocean. I think there's something fishy there." He laughed at his own pun but Kirsten barely smiled. "Want another hamburger?"

"Heavens no, I'm stuffed now."

Back at Stevenson House Manuel let her scramble off the motorcycle by herself saying, "'Bye, Kirsten, I'm late."

"Not very polite," she thought, glad of his faults.

She turned in at the front door of the museum. Her aunt was out of sight, talking to a group of tourists. Kirsten could hear her special public voice saying, "This is the Buddha that Stevenson kept on his writing table in Samoa to bring him luck. We think this brass temple bell was used to call the family to prayers."

Coming back to the reception room, Grace smiled a welcome. "Hello, Kirsten. I'm not very busy today."

"I went for a ride on Manuel's motorcycle."

"Yes, I saw you."

The tourists had gone through the front hall and could be heard on the groaning boards overhead. Grace sat down at the desk. "I'm trying to decide whether to talk to the police again," she said. "I'm sick about the things that are disappearing here."

"What now?"

"A gold thimble. I know it was on the ivory spindle on that French sewing table when I closed up last night. This morning—gone, before anyone had come."

"I tell you, Aunt Grace, things are spirited away."

"Besides that, one of the prettiest things anyone has ever given us—a tiny Scotch bagpipe with a silver chanter. I had it pinned to a doll in the children's room. That's gone too."

"What's a chanter?"

"It's the melody pipe on a bagpipe."

It was soon after the last of the tourists had left that the wailing began upstairs. Grace and Kirsten looked at each other and with one accord hurried to the front hall. Kirsten raced up the stairs ahead of her aunt and ran along the hall to the children's room at the end.

"It seemed to come from here," she called as Grace panted after her, "but it's all quiet now. Come on," she said with an attempt at courage, "let's search through all the rooms."

The whole floor reminded her poignantly of her first night here. There was a musty smell of ancient fabrics; and she felt the sadness of lives that had been lived here and were forever gone.

Her aunt pointed to the ancient sewing machine in the tiny room at the head of the stairs. "A seamstress used to come once a year," she said, "and make clothes for all the women in the household. In Monterey they always called her 'the sewing woman.' She sewed one week for the women, then one week for the men. There were few tailors in those days. This trousseau was lent to us by an old Monterey family, whose daughter was married during the time Stevenson lived here."

Kirsten tried to imagine the joy of that bride now dead. But the satin wedding gown on the dress form looked dingy and yellow. Dust streaks had formed in the gathers of the high puffed sleeves. And the bride's purple traveling dress with its long full skirt and endless yards of black braid was so old-fashioned it made her want to cry. She found more pleasure in the tiny replicas of these garments hanging on a line. They had obviously been made for the china-headed doll in the corner.

Her aunt moved on to the door of the parlor. "This is where the gold thimble was," she said, "on that sewing table. The widow of Juan Girardin lived here when Stevenson rented the back bedroom. That tip-top table belonged to Stevenson himself. Come on, let's walk around the rooms. But don't walk on that Spanish rug. It's so old it shouldn't be on the floor."

Grace opened the lock of the waist-high gate and Kirsten followed her into the room. The girl counted three bell glasses protecting sea shell flowers. Between the tall front windows a mirrored what-not held spread fans, sea shells, and vases. Kirsten imagined Mama Girardin sitting on the green couch talking over the day's events with her children's nurse while Stevenson played bezique with her young son, and the girls counted sea shells on the rug. She was sure that in the old days a Chinese jardiniere had stood in a corner holding pampas grass and peacock feathers.

Her aunt had gone on into the next room and Kirsten followed, peering at the high spool bed covered with a finely quilted white spread and snowy pillow shams. A hooded cradle stood beside it, and curling irons hung in the lamp chimney beside a washbowl and pitcher on a marble-topped dresser. An embroidered long-sleeved night-gown lay across a padded rocker. Everything looked as if someone were going to bed in a few minutes.

Suddenly from the corner wardrobe came a scratching and snarling sound that made Kirsten jump. But Grace calmly went over and threw open the door of the wardrobe. "That darn cat again! It belongs to Jane. It comes over sometimes in Mr. Tinsley's pickup. Get out. Scat!"

The cat ran yowling.

63

"How will it get out?" said Kirsten.

"Oh, she has her own entrance in the broom closet downstairs. She spends a lot of time under the house. Once she raised three kittens there."

"That could be the ghost," said Kirsten brightly.

"And turn down the covers of a bed and steal things? Hah!"

"Then we're right back to a mysterious person."

Grace put a hand to her forehead. "Let's just forget the ghost for now, Kirsten. It really gives me a headache."

"I tell you what," said Kirsten. "You lie down while I make Scotch woodcock for supper and then we'll go for a walk."

"Scotch woodcock?"

"You know—onions and cheese, tomatoes and egg, all scrambled up together."

"Sounds wonderful. Come on."

After they had stacked the dishes in the sink they walked down Alvarado Street toward the Wharf, the same way Kirsten and Jane had gone that morning. But how different it was now! No young men followed them nor did they stop to look in the stores.

"We'll go up to Presidio Hill," said Grace. "There's a good view of the bay from there." She walked briskly and Kirsten set her pace to match the older woman's.

"There's the first brick house built in California," pointed out her aunt. "Built in 1847. And this is the site of the old whaling station. Monterey was a whaling center in the nineteenth century."

They waited for several minutes for the heavy traffic to slow up, then crossed to the foot of Presidio Hill and plodded up to its crest. From here they could see the brilliant colors of Fisherman's Wharf and the darkening bay to the north.

"There was a Chinese fishing village there till it burned in 1906," said Grace.

"And before that?"

"Well, Cabrillo saw the bay first in 1542; and it was another sixty years before Vizcaino landed and named this place Monterey. It means king of the mountain."

"I thought this was all begun by Father—what do they call him?—Juniper'o Serra."

"Hu–nip–ero. It's Spanish. No, he came in 1770. He founded ten missions in California." Under a big oak near the hilltop they found the stone image of Father Serra stepping from a boat, dressed in robe and surplice and holding a Bible.

Finally they stood beside the wooden cross on the very top of the hill. Three cannons on concrete supports were at their feet and planes flew overhead. Buses and cars swept around the foot of the hill on their way to Pacific Grove and Carmel.

The sun was setting as they retraced their steps down to the city. They could hear the barking sea lions beyond Cannery Row and the guns booming at Fort Ord.

But it was not of ancient history that Kirsten was thinking as they walked slowly back up Alvarado Street toward the museum. "Aunt Grace," she said in a troubled voice so low her aunt had to bend to hear, "what would you do if you thought you loved two men at once?"

They walked in step for a moment, then Grace said, "Why, my dear, I'd wait for a third one to come along."

7

Kirsten answered a knock at the door next morning to find Jane and a new young man. Her first impression of Harry Andrews was that he was indeed, as Jane and Manuel had said, a thoroughly nice person. He was very tall and slender, what any Ohioan would call a bean pole. His crew cut was bright red and he wore thick-lensed glasses.

"He does have beautiful white teeth," Kirsten thought charitably, "and a nice smile."

Jane was wearing a pair of faded jeans cut off raggedly at the knees, a bright red cotton shirt, and a straw hat. Harry carried three fishing rods and wore baggy khaki work pants and a white T-shirt.

"We've come to take you fishing," announced Jane. "It's Harry's morning off. Harry even remembered to bring his sister's license for you."

Kirsten ran a hand over her hair, hoping she had combed

it right. She was glad she had put on her pink voile dress. Jane reached out a hand and touched her cheek. "Kirstie," she cried, "you look beautiful. Your skin is so clear. It's—"

"It's what?"

"Your—you know—acne, it's practically gone."

Kirsten could have choked her. To have that mentioned at a time like this! "Well, hurray for our side," she said.

"It must be that powdered yeast your aunt gives you. Come on now, get into your slacks."

Kirsten changed into black slacks and a pink-striped T-shirt.

"Here," groaned Jane as Kirsten came back into the living room, "wipe off that red lipstick and use my pink. Good heavens!"

"How many colors do you carry?" marveled Harry.

"Got bait?" asked Kirsten as they clattered down the steps.

"We buy squid at the pier."

"Where are we going?"

"Municipal Pier. I've been fishing there ever since I was four," said Harry. "My Dad used to help me straighten out the points of the starfish I caught. They're thick on the piles under water. We'd let them dry on the pier and carry them home. Dad put a plate rail in my bedroom and finally I had starfish all around me, all four walls with a frieze of starfish. It began to smell pretty fishy after a while."

Jane shuddered. "Harry, how awful! You never told me that."

"I didn't think you'd care much for my starfish."

"I've got used to an awful lot of fish talk from you over the years," she reminded him. "Remember when you entered the fishing derby and got the heaviest ling cod last summer? Are you still wearing the prize?"

"Sure." Harry beamed and held out his wrist toward Kirsten, displaying a handsome gold watch. "This year there's a grand prize for the largest salmon caught by Labor Day—a boat with motor and trailer. I won the weekly cash prize last week—seven fifty for a white sea bass. It was only seven pounds but the largest taken all week."

Jane danced along the streets in a merry mood that made Kirsten feel inadequate. "What's the matter, Kirsten?" Jane asked. "Homesick?"

"No, not really. It's just—I don't know—I feel sad, that's all. I wish Roger were here."

"Well, natch—seeing as you're engaged to him."

Kirsten saw the quick glance Harry gave her, but he didn't say anything. They bought the bait and walked out on the long pier past parked trucks and jeeps. In the sunny lee of the packing shed, old brown fishermen were skillfully mending the rust-colored nets heaped around them. Scattered among the nets were cork floats, round as doughnuts. Several hundred fishing craft, white and blue and gleaming with polished brass, rocked gently in the harbor.

The three friends settled down at the end of the pier. Jane promptly backlashed her line when she cast out and begged Harry's help in untangling it and winding it back on the reel. Kirsten looked at her knowingly but said nothing.

Staring down between the piles, Kirsten saw a huge jellyfish like a transparent lavender umbrella gliding through the water far below. She pointed it out to Harry.

He nodded. "Out in the bay jellyfish are a real problem for the small boats," he said. "You can't troll where there are very many."

Gradually Kirsten became aware of several small sleek round heads watching her from the water. They seemed to be forming a wide semicircle around the fishermen on the pier. She caught Harry's amused glance and laughed. "We're being spied on."

"Sea lions," he laughed. "They come over from the breakwater. There's a colony of them over there, must be hundreds, counting the babies. I must take you over there some time. It's a treat to see them."

Harry was silent for a moment as he watched Jane reel in her line. She shook her head and grinned. "False alarm."

Kirsten was not particularly excited when she pulled in several small bocaccio, but Jane gave a happy scream over her single catch—which she made Harry remove. He caught eight. They gave them all to a small Japanese boy, who already had a gunnysackful.

At eleven Jane announced, "I want a pizza, Harry."

"Oh, you and your appetite!"

"Don't you, Kirstie?" Jane pleaded.

"Well, whenever I think about Aunt Grace's powdered yeast . . ."

"Come on, then," Jane said, jumping up.

When they had sat down in the bright pink pizza shop, Harry pulled out his wallet to look at the single bill inside.

"Dutch treat," said Kirsten firmly, and Jane added, "Let's have one among us, with everything on."

While they ate Jane chattered about the boys and girls she and Harry knew in their high school class. They seemed no different from her own classmates in Ohio, thought Kirsten. She had never fit in there until she had become engaged to Roger. Then suddenly they had both been accepted. No longer had she been a fifth wheel, and it had been so good to belong!

Jane laughed. "Kirstie is thinking of her O and O."

"O and O?"

"One and only."

Deliberately Kirsten brought her mind back to the problems of the present. She told Harry about all the eerie happenings at Stevenson House and the things that had been stolen. "Someone must have it in for my aunt, though I can't imagine who."

Jane said teasingly, "So you've quit believing in ghosts."

Kirsten nodded. She was a little tired of the light manner in which both Jane and Manuel joked about the ghost. She wanted her friends to help her track down the trouble. She looked across at Harry and saw that he was folding and refolding his paper napkin, concentrating on her words.

This was a boy who thought not just of himself and his

crowd, but even of the problems of an adult like her aunt and of a stranger like herself.

Jane wiped her fingers daintily on a napkin. "Come on, Dad will be in a tizzy if I'm not back by twelve."

"Some time when I have a morning off," said Harry, when they had reached the gate of Stevenson House, "maybe you'd like to explore the tide pools down the coast. That's my favorite occupation, Kirstie."

"Maybe Manuel could go too," said Kirsten hesitantly.

Jane gave her a searching look. "He might have to bring his little brother."

"Well, that would be all right. Louis is lonely. See you around."

That afternoon Kirsten decided to make cookies. At home, whenever she was soul-hungry or just plain hungry, she went into the kitchen and mixed up a batch of cookies.

"I'll make dream bars," she said, digging out a recipe she had copied from her aunt's filing cabinet. "Have to go to the store for coconut and brown sugar." She combed her hair more carefully than usual and put on fresh lipstick. Then she crossed the back garden and went through the big wooden gate to the supermarket on Munras Avenue.

Harry was at the check-out counter. Kirsten found the things she needed as quickly as possible and waited until he was free to check her groceries, though two other clerks stood idle.

"Hi," he said. "You're a pretty good fisherman."

"Thanks. So's Jane, though she did backlash her line."

He nodded. "Jane likes a man to wait on her. It's her idea of being feminine."

"She's fun though."

A man cleared his throat and Kirsten was suddenly aware of a line of customers waiting behind her. She picked up her package and went out of the store.

When she had finished making the cookies it was so hot that she threw open the two front windows. And in a few

minutes she heard childish voices down below. "Hey, lady up there."

She did not recognize the two little wide-eyed boys. Their ears flared pink in the sunlight and they reached up their hands. "It smells good—like cookies. Can we have some?"

"They're not out of the pan yet. Come on up."

When she opened the door Louis Castro was with them. He looked dirtier than ever, and he stood rubbing the instep of one bare foot with the sole of the other. "I'm hungry too," he said.

She looked at the two young strangers. "I don't think I know you." She hesitated to ask them in.

"Our father is Max Weidman, the ranger. He came over to see your aunt about somethin'. We're Jock and Harold."

"Come in. I'm just going to cut the cookies."

They stood so close that she could barely wield the knife. Kirsten gently sawed through the crumbly crust in each tin. The smell of coconut and brown sugar poured through the cut, and the boys breathed it in eagerly. Jock danced up and down.

"There is nothing so good in all the world," thought Kirsten, "as having just made something to eat and having children around you begging for it."

"You'd better eat them outside," she advised, looking at her aunt's immaculate room. But Louis had already begun to wolf down his cookie. She saw shreds of coconut around his bare feet, and so did he. He plumped down on his hands and knees and, licking a forefinger repeatedly, he applied it to each shred of coconut.

"Maybe you'd like another," she said, looking into his black eyes.

"Two more," said Louis.

Their fists were full, their faces beaming as they turned to go back downstairs. Kirsten helped herself to a cookie and ate it dreamily. "What makes Manuel so appealing," she thought, "is having a young brother like that. Louis ought to play with those Weidman boys. Why is he such a little lone wolf, I wonder."

That night as they sat in the living room, Kirsten and her aunt heard a loud creaking noise on the porch. "Ghosts walking," said Grace with a nervous smile. But when they heard a swishing sound against the wall beside the door, Grace held her breath for a moment and then went to the door and unlocked and unlatched all four of the bars she maintained against intruders.

She threw open the door and stepped outside, looking down into the back garden. There was no one, nothing! Then suddenly from the Stevenson bedroom they heard the sound of furniture being moved. And as they clutched each other in terror there was music.

"I'm going across and see," said Grace, and bravely crossed the porch. She peered into the bedroom and tried the door, but found it locked.

Kirsten was puzzled. "But why didn't the burglar alarm go off?"

"I don't know." Grace angrily shook the door a moment longer.

She returned to Kirsten, who stood trembling in the lighted doorway of the apartment. "Whoever our ghost is must have been scraping those chairs around in front of the fireplace, but they're back in place now and there isn't a sound inside. This is going to drive me mad." She went into her bedroom and returned with a flashlight and the keys to the museum.

"Aunt Grace, you aren't going in there now!"

"Indeed I am!"

"But suppose—just suppose this is a—a dangerous character?"

Her aunt was not listening. She had unlocked the door and in high dudgeon had marched into the Stevenson bedroom. She peered under the bed and went into the other rooms, waving the flashlight. There was no one there.

She was very grumpy when she came back out and relocked the bedroom door. "I don't want to talk about it," she said with finality. "I'll phone the police tomorrow."

By the next morning Grace had recovered her usual good spirits. "Kirsten, today I'm going over to Asilomar to hear some free music. Want to come along?"

"Free music?"

"Yes. There's a three-day session of symphony conductors studying there. They conduct groups of musicians in the chapel and welcome audiences to hear their work. I go every summer. It's a beautiful place, a state park. Then this afternoon we could go for a walk if you'd like."

Kirsten felt as if she should be her aunt's companion, but there was a chance Manuel would stop by. "I don't think so, Aunt Grace. But thanks." She realized her aunt was disappointed and she felt guilty. What kind of peculiar spell was she under?

When Grace went down to the desk to call the police, Kirsten went along to meet Max Weidman, Grace's substitute for the day. He was, she thought, the largest man she had ever seen. He was tall and powerfully built, with heavy brows over exceedingly bright blue eyes. He held out his hand.

"My boys tell me you're a good cook. I'm afraid they've dubbed you 'cookie lady.' "

"I don't mind." Kirsten rubbed the fingers of the hand he had gripped. "They're nice boys. You didn't bring them today."

"No, their mother took them to a swimming class over in Pacific Grove."

"I wish Louis would go along."

Mr. Weidman chuckled. "He could stand a little water."

Kirsten spoke sharply in her distress. "He could stand being with boys his own age too."

Max sobered. "I know. My wife and I have often talked about that. He's wild, that one. She's asked him to come over to our house but he won't do it."

"Shy," said Kirsten.

Manuel came as Grace was leaving. He was just suggesting a walk to Kirsten when he was interrupted by the gay voice, of Jane. "Hi, anyone here?" And the girl was there in the doorway, bathed in light and prettier than ever in an apple-green dress. Kirsten watched Manuel's delighted glance and recalled the joy she had felt when Roger had joined her in a crowd. Even the pain she had felt at his last letter disappeared, though it had been intense when she read, "Lorna tells me you see a lot of someone named Manuel. She broke a date the other night and went to a movie with me."

"Maybe Jane will come with us," said Manuel.

"Oh, let's sit under the magnolia tree and talk," countered Jane. "I feel lazy this morning."

Kirsten remembered the time only a fortnight ago when she had sat here with Manuel and they had told each other all about themselves. Now it was different. Jane was never serious with a boy. She set up a defense of double meanings, a bantering that skipped brightly over their talk like a rock skimming the surface of a pool. She teased Manuel about the girls they both knew, and Kirsten had a feeling *she* was being told Manuel could not possibly be interested in her.

She withdrew into herself and sat silent. Fog was still in the treetops and she could hear a far barking and a farther booming and thought, "That's the old sea lion at Fisherman's Wharf. And those are the guns at Fort Ord."

The other two did not miss her when she went around to the front gate for the mail. There was only a circular and a bill for her aunt. Despondently she picked up one of the abalone shells that edged the garden walk. Its inward curving surface held a rainbow. She told herself she loved and was loved, but her heart ached.

She put the shell back in its place and straightened up to look into the sky. Above the fog were blue hills, tree-fringed, cupping the town and the bay. She looked at Stevenson House, wondering at its strange power to evoke ghostly images.

Then she saw Louis. He was standing by the picket gate

watching her. She wished she dared tell Manuel that he neglected his brother.

"Aren't you cold, Louis?" she said noticing that he wore only the usual faded overall.

"Naw, I'm used to this weather. It's always foggy in the morning. I just come over to see if Manuel was here. Now I'm goin' down to the beach."

"Can I go with you?"

Louis looked at her in surprise. "I thought Manuel and you were goin' some place."

"He won't miss me," she answered. "He's with Jane."

Near the beach Louis pointed to a narrow yellow two-story house in a street of shabby run-down buildings. Tall anise weeds grew around the house. "That's where I live," he said, "second floor."

Kirsten looked at the curtainless narrow windows and imagined the life Manuel and Louis must have there. No wonder Manuel treasured his motorcycle, a beautiful shining object that would bear him away from such a place. No wonder Louis read incessantly in the evenings and wandered everywhere all day in a soiled overall.

She felt a surge of pity for them both.

8

Kirsten stood looking into the mirror above her dresser. "Your eyes are your best feature," Jane had said. Kirsten was sure Jane was right about everything relating to a girl's appearance. She ran her hand over her hair, pushing the bangs down past her heavy eyebrows. "They'll have to be trimmed. They've already grown too long."

She wished she could have hair like Jane's. Perhaps if she dyed hers blond? No, not unless Jane said so. Jane would know. Jane could even see at a glance when a lipstick shade was wrong. She was a marvel about looking just right.

But it was not because of Jane that Kirsten's eyes gazed into her reflection. Accusingly she said to her image, "You are neglecting your aunt and she paid for you to come out here. You're having fun with Manuel and Jane and Harry. But what about Aunt Grace? You let her go away alone yesterday and you were punished by having a rotten time yourself."

Restlessly she turned from the mirror as she heard the bathroom door open. "I'll take my shower now and have breakfast with her. We can make some plans. I'd help her with that old ghost if I had the faintest notion how to go about it. But maybe since it's at the bottom of my mind all the time, and especially whenever I'm in the museum, I'll get a clue when I least expect it."

At breakfast she said, "Aunt Grace, I want to go on a history walk with you next time you go."

Her aunt's open pleasure gave her heart a lift. "Good. I don't want to take you away from your friends though. How about today?"

"Today! But yesterday you were off."

"Darling, you've really been in a fog since you came. I have two free days a week. On Wednesday Mr. Weidman takes my place at the desk. On Thursday the place is closed."

"I sort of wondered a couple of days why there were so few people around."

"Few! None except us and the gardener and the janitor."

Kirsten had hardly been able to tell one day from another since she came. Sunday, always special at home by reason of dressing for church and having dinner at one o'clock, was an extra busy workday here.

"If the Custom House is open today I'd like to see it," she said.

"Good." Grace poured another cup of coffee. "Since it doesn't open till nine we'll have time to walk up to the Royal Presidio Chapel first. I'd like you to see everything in case this is your only visit to Monterey."

"My only . . ." Kirsten took a quick gulp of coffee.

"Oh, impossible!" she told herself. "Why, I'm just beginning to know this place! But what if she's right, and I never come again?"

78

Monterey had an early-morning look; moisture still lay on the roofs and walls and flowers. As they passed a garden behind a gray paling fence, Grace seized Kirsten's hand.

"Look, honey—carnations, Esther Reed daisies, asters—"

"I can't tell one flower from another," admitted Kirsten. "Except roses."

"Well, they're good to start on. Here we are."

Kirsten looked up at an old adobe church, whose red tile roof glowed, even in the foggy air. Two crosses on the façade thrust upward into the sky. Beyond the church to the left was a dark grove of olive trees and second growth redwoods.

"We won't go in," said Grace. "There are early morning communicants. One thing I never could stand in the cathedrals of Europe were the gawking sight-seers being lectured in the midst of worshipers. But I do want you to see the grotto, it's a copy of the one at Lourdes."

The statue of the Virgin Mary stood in a corner of the churchyard. They sat down on a bench in the dank and dusky peace. Kirsten reached out her hand to touch a small heart of white marble set into the stone. It bore the carved word "Merci."

"Someone thanking the Virgin for a cure from heart disease," whispered Grace.

"Or maybe heartbreak," thought Kirsten.

"Come on, dear, it will be nine by the time we walk down to the Custom House. Max Weidman is in charge there. Maybe he'll offer us a cup of coffee."

Kirsten had passed the Custom House when she had gone to Fisherman's Wharf with Jane and again when she and Grace had gone up to Presidio Hill. It faced the water front and had an open verandah two stories high, extending up to the Spanish tile roof. In the walled yard pepper trees hung their rosy berries above old weathered benches, and round beds of cacti were edged with abalone shells. Against the front verandah leaned a six-foot bronze anchor from some long-gone ship.

"It's the oldest government building west of the Rocky Mountains," said Grace. "It was built during the Mexican period. John Drake Sloat raised the flag here in 1846."

Inside at the desk sat Max Weidman, pouring coffee from a Thermos bottle into a plastic cup.

"Grace! And Kirsten! Welcome. I thought you'd never get around to my old Custom House." He rose and held out his hand. "Have some coffee?"

"We'd have been here before but Kirsten is just too popular. Thanks, I'll have a cup."

Smiling, Kirsten shook her head. "I'll look around. I love old costumes."

Leaving Grace and Max, the girl slipped upstairs. Puzzled by a case of decorated eggs she stopped to read about them:

"Monterey was famous for its *Bailes de los Cascarones*. These were public dances using *cascarones* (eggshells) as favors. A *cascarón* was filled with colored paper from China and gold leaf cut into confetti. Paper was then pasted over the hole at the end. Sometimes these shells were filled with cologne; at times even with pure gold dust."

Kirsten continued reading with growing excitement: "Baskets of *cascarones* were taken to the dances, where the custom was to hold the *cascarón* over the head of a favored señorita and crush the shell so that the confetti floated down on her hair. *Cascarón* balls were especially popular just before Lent, and quantities were on hand for the festivities of the Christmas season."

"Now wouldn't that be an idea!" marveled Kirsten. Her mind drifted into a happy daydream of a dance in Rockland with Roger crushing a *cascarón* of rose fragrance over her hair. "What a crazy notion!" She shook her head. Against her will the thought came, "But Manuel would do it and think it was fun." And then full-blown came her inspiration, "I could tell him and Jane about it. We could plan a surprise dance for Aunt Grace for the end of the summer, just before I leave. We needn't tell her until we have all the arrangements made. It would be a grand thing to look forward to—and to look back on when I've gone home again."

Hugging her secret idea and feeling happier than she had since she came to Monterey, she rejoined her aunt.

"Where to now?" Kirsten said brightly.

"I was just looking at Max's bus schedule," Grace said. "We could take a bus out to Asilomar for a concert. There's a practice session for one of the state college orchestras at eleven. Do you like Wagner? They're doing parts of *The Flying Dutchman*. Then we could have lunch in the dining room on the grounds. They have a Chinese cook and the most heavenly homemade bread."

"I'd love that, though frankly I don't know *The Flying Dutchman*. I just know tag ends of Wagner's music."

"You'll have to hurry," said Max, "or you'll miss the bus."

Kirsten felt a wave of affection for her aunt. She looked at her as they sat on the bus. She saw a woman still pretty and vital. "The same bright blue eyes as Dad's," she thought, "but she can dress much better than my mother, even though Mom does sew so well. The word for Aunt Grace is chic."

"You're not listening to a word I say," scolded Grace.

"You're trying to tell me the names of all the flowers." Kirsten laughed. "I told you it's no use. All I will remember is their colors—bright pink and blue and lots of purple. And those orange flowers on the trees—eucalyptus? But I do know grass when I see it, and I never saw such brilliant lawns."

"Yes, the fog is good for something."

"Do you suppose it's possible to fall in love with a *place*, Aunt Grace?"

"It's been done."

As the bus turned a corner, Kirsten read a sign beside the road. "Butterfly trees!" she exclaimed. "Now I've heard everything. What in the world is a butterfly tree?"

"There are quite a few of them around here where monarch butterflies settle by the millions after the middle of October. Any tree will do, so long as it's in this area. There are scattered trees in Pacific Grove and Carmel and Monterey where they settle. I can't tell you why. It's an amazing sight, thrilling really."

"Where do they come from?"

"As far away as Alaska. They seem to have fly-ways just as migrating birds do. In summer they have to live where there is milkweed. That's the only thing they eat."

"I'd like to see them."

"Come again and stay through October." This was the second time that day that Grace had referred to Kirsten's leaving at the end of the summer.

The bus turned in at the gates of Asilomar State Park and rumbled over a narrow road, winding between slender trees. The driver parked before the stone administration building facing a ring of beautifully contorted Monterey pines. As they climbed off the bus, Grace said, "There's no time now for a walk, but I am filled with shame to think you haven't really seen the sea since you came."

"But Monterey Bay—"

"I mean the breakers, the ocean. We'll walk down to the shore after lunch. If only I didn't work on Sunday I'd have some of my friends take us on the Seventeen Mile Drive and down to Big Sur."

"Well, perhaps a hint to Manuel—"

"On that motorcycle? Not on your life, girl. I'll talk to Harry. He has a car—of sorts."

Kirsten looked around eagerly. The buildings were simple and Japanesque, set among dark trees that had been blown by ocean winds into forms of great beauty. Atop the hills and in the woods she could see the brown Long Houses, and the guest houses of more gracious appearance.

They walked toward the redwood chapel, where a great busyness of tuning up was taking place. Kirsten loved the cacophony, the sight of the symphonic instruments—even though she knew all too little about music. Perhaps this was a gap in her life she could yet fill, she thought, for once glad that she was only seventeen.

Behind the stage where the orchestra played was a floor-to-roof window. Three crooked old pines in the white dunes stretched their horizontal branches across a sky that changed from white to blue as the fog cleared and the sun came out.

As the music poured over and through her, Kirsten hoped she would carry this picture with her always.

After lunch they walked through the harsh sea grass to the dunes, then along a path between great patches of bright red sedums and yellow and lavender sand verbena. Kirsten could not take her eyes away from the wide sweep of white sand to the north, where the endless blue waves laid down scallops of white foam.

"Look, Aunt Grace, there are some surfers!"

"Yes, I'm told the boys do most of the surfing. The girls sit on the sand and admire them."

Kirsten and Grace sat on a tall dune where they could look out to the sea and took off their shoes and stockings. Thrusting their toes deep into the cool damp sand, they fell into a companionable silence.

9

The magnolia tree in the pearly morning light looked like a painting on white satin. A few white buds drank in the fog. Kirsten felt that she too drank it in and knew that she would always love fog.

"Some do and some don't." She smiled and knew that if Jane had said that she would instantly have capped it with the words, "to coin a phrase." Aunt Grace disliked the fog and had several times complained bitterly that July and August were not good months in Monterey.

"July begins today," Kirsten reminded herself. She heard the shower and roused herself to close the window and go out to start the coffee. Then she would have time to shower and dress while Grace prepared the eggs and toast.

"We work well together," thought Kirsten. "I *am* going to do something for Aunt Grace. She's done so much for me.

I'm going to give her a surprise ball at the end of my visit, a *Baile de los Cascarones*. I'll get the others to help."

She eagerly awaited the arrival of her three friends; it was time again for Harry's half day off. Soon after Grace had gone to work Kirsten heard Jane's step on the stairs. She opened the door and her eyes stopped with shock on Manuel.

He had had his hair cut short and combed from a side part like Roger's. And his cheeks and chin were smooth and beardless. He was dressed in a dark brown shirt and slacks.

"Oh, Manuel!" she cried and put her palms against her cheeks in a gesture of disbelief.

"Doesn't he look great, Kirstie?" Jane beamed. "I told you I'm champion haircutter in this vicinity. Look how good I made *you* look."

"Already," answered Kirsten tartly, "my bangs need cutting. I can see this hair business runs into money."

"Not while you have me around. But I mustn't kid you, I didn't cut Manuel's hair."

"She sure talked me into it though," he said.

"We thought you might like to go surfing," said Jane. "Harry's got an extra surfboard."

"What a coincidence! Aunt Grace and I were watching the surfers at Asilomar yesterday. She said mostly the fellows ride the boards and the girls watch."

"You just watch this girl," Jane laughed. "Come on, our bathing suits are in Harry's car. We go to Pacific Grove. We can change in the dressing rooms there by the pool."

Apparently Jane was still Harry's date—despite the obvious glances of interest exchanged between her and Manuel—for she climbed into the front seat while Manuel helped Kirsten into the back. But as they drove along Manuel talked constantly to Jane and he finally leaned forward and put his finger through a curl beside her ear. She slapped his hand but did not look displeased. Kirsten felt herself slipping back into her old unhappiness, her old uncertainty. Would

anyone except Roger ever look at her the way Manuel looked at Jane?

They parked the car at Lovers Point and got the surf-boards out of the trunk. As they went down the wide stone stairs to the beach, Kirsten was bumped by a young man clad all in black rubber, with large flapping rubber fins on his feet.

"Bruce!" said Jane. "I didn't know you'd taken up scuba diving. How are you?"

"Hi, Jane! Hey, Manuel, who got *you* down in a barber's chair?"

He passed on then to catch up with another black neptune on the shore, calling back, "Got a job. Matt and I swim under the glass-bottomed boat every trip. Not bad pay and fun for us."

Kirsten's heart sank. "Don't tell me I have to learn scuba diving too," she groaned.

Harry gave her arm a reassuring squeeze. "No, that's not for you Kirstie."

When they had all put on their swim suits, Kirsten followed Jane's instructions and example. Holding on to her surfboard, she trod the sand through the shallow water, slid onto the board, and paddled out beyond the breakers.

Tremendous skill was needed to slide onto the board, she discovered. She tried to stand upright, spreading her feet to balance and glide in to shore on the treacherously play-ful waves. It had looked so easy yesterday. Jane told her to wait for the seventh wave, she said it was always an extra large one.

Kirsten did not count her failures, for she knew herself to be easily discouraged. But she was sure that a dozen times she fell off her board and thrashed angrily in the water while the other three assumed an easy and graceful stance, gliding out of the sea toward the shore.

But at last Kirsten made it shakily upright. And suddenly she had the feeling of being one with the board as it slid with a wave toward the beach ahead. She and the water and the sky were one beautiful flowing movement. "Glorious!" she thought when her board bumped bottom and she leaped into the foam.

Manuel was beside her and his bright black eyes were merry. "You are a sport, Kirsten," he said.

The ache she had felt when she watched him with Jane in the car eased. "It's enough to be liked," she thought. Then she reminded herself crossly, "Besides, I am loved. Roger loves me." Aloud she said, "Is there time for a few more?"

But Jane had darted to where she could see the clock above the boat dock. "Oh golly, we've got to hurry or I'll never make it back by noon. And you know my dad."

"We do," answered Harry grimly. "And I have to get to work."

"Well, look." Manuel had seized Kirsten's hand. "I don't have to be at work till four. I want to take this gal in the glass-bottomed boat. We don't often get this much sun, and that's when the bottom is pretty. Jane, you tell her aunt I'll have her back on the two o'clock bus, okay?"

Kirsten rejoiced in the fact that Jane looked disgruntled. "Do her good," she thought.

Watching Harry and Jane push through the sand back to the car she remembered that she had meant to talk to them about a surprise ball. Well, that could wait. It was so gratifying to have Manuel want to stay on with her. She was aware of all the other people on the beach sunning themselves, watching little children tumble into and out of the water, sometimes going in for a dip but mostly moving as little as possible.

"Everyone's rejoicing in a morning of sun," said Manuel. "Do you want a hot dog, or would you rather go up to the restaurant by the highway and have some abalone chowder?"

"Well . . ."

"I know. You'd rather have the chowder but you don't know how much money I have." His eyes crinkled. "For

your information I was paid yesterday. Let's have the chowder."

They shared a table in the crowded dining room. As soon as they were seated, Kirsten launched into her plans for the ball. "Manuel, I had the most marv inspiration yesterday . . ."

It was just as she had imagined—Manuel knew all about *cascarones*. He approved of her idea and suggested she discuss it with Max Weidman. "He knows all the people who have state building jobs and the people who act in the Old Theater—in fact, all your aunt's friends. Even a few rich biddies who have places near Pebble Beach. More coffee?"

"Oh, I'm so glad you like the idea, Manuel," Kirsten said. "It's a perfectly gorgeous day after all."

"Come on, we can catch the next boat. It's a perfect day for you to see the bottom," Manuel said.

Kirsten followed him out into the bright blue day and down the wide steps to the boat landing. When the passengers were seated around the glass opening in the bottom of the boat, curtains were lowered so that the only light came through the window looking into the ocean.

The boat began to move slowly out from the landing and Kirsten caught her breath at the beauty gliding before her eyes. Broad-leaved kelp moved and swayed beneath the boat, curling and waving softly with its passage. The kelp was copper-colored with rainbow surfaces. It was bronze-green, like khaki. There was a lacy lavender variety that curved as gracefully as a dancer. And it all mingled with bright-green eelgrass that looked like long green hair. No wonder mermaids had grown out of man's imagination. And there to remind her of mermen, were the two scuba divers, cavorting and grinning up at the people in the boat.

"Fun, Kirsten?" Manuel asked.

"Wonderful."

"Like a technicolor movie, isn't it?"

She wished Harry were there to tell her the names of all

the things she saw. Now she could see tiny white baby starfish lying on the lavender kelp like five-petaled spring flowers. Starfish of all colors lay on the hilly white sand floor—white, black, lavender, but mostly orange. She recognized the spiked sea urchins and the soft pastels of sea anemones.

"It's like an oriental rug, isn't it?" said Manuel.

"I hadn't thought of it that way, Manuel. How far are we from shore?"

"We're quite close. We're at the base of those gray cliffs we saw on our way back from the restaurant. The ocean floor's about thirty feet down."

When they came out into the sunshine at the end of an unbelievable hour, Kirsten said, "I'll never make a surface judgment on anything or anyone again."

Manuel squeezed her hand responsively. "Yes, you never know when you meet someone what prickly sea urchins are buried in the canyons of his soul."

"Oh, Manuel," said Kirsten, "that's exactly what I meant."

She had come to dread the mail from her parents because she knew there would be no mention of Roger among all the trivia they discussed. She felt as though she were leading a split life, one part devoted to Roger—much the smaller part. Her father's postcards, studiedly casual, made her feel that Roger did not exist at all. And her mother's letters mentioned him but conveyed only distress:

Roger came out last night to see if we had heard from you! Lorna was hanging around so he took her downtown for a soda, I think! All the kids send their heartiest hugs and say to tell you the cookies are eaten up!

Her mother's letters were always as studded with exclamation marks as are landscapes with telephone poles. Kirsten longed for her father to write, "We hope you are getting over your intention to marry Roger. You are too immature for marriage." Then she could answer, respectful and re-spected, yet protected from making the decision herself, "Yes, I believe I am."

But all her father wrote was, "Arnold lost a tooth today and the fairies left a quarter—inflation!" And at the end of the letter, "We hope some nice boys are not too far distant from Stevenson House. But we hope too that you keep your distance!"

"Oh, Daddy, your heavy humor!" thought Kirsten. "No chance the boys will bother me while Jane is around."

She marveled constantly at Jane's boundless energy, at her total enthusiasm directed toward anything from food to sweaters, to records, to surfing and swimming, and back again to food. Only two things Jane would not do: be late for her afternoon with her mother or ride behind Manuel on his motorcycle.

"We're all going tide pooling at Point Joe," said Harry one morning, fitting his long body behind the steering wheel of his car. "The tide will be just right by the time we get there."

"Take me anywhere so long as it's to the ocean," said Kirsten and was gratified by her friends' laughter. She thought she would never tire of the trip down past the old Custom House along the highway at the base of Presidio Hill, then right through Cannery Row and continuing along the bay shore through Pacific Grove. They passed Lovers Point and went on to the rolling dunes from which they could see the horizontal pine boughs of Asilomar.

Harry pulled off the highway beside a cluster of granite boulders that thrust up like a castle between road and sea. They climbed out of the car and scrambled down close to the water, Manuel going ahead and reaching up to help the girls. Harry carried a Thermos jug of cider and a paper bag of cups and doughnuts.

"Here's the place for soul searching, Kirstie," said Jane.

Kirsten looked at the ocean silently until Harry nudged her and pointed to the blanket spread on the sand. She dropped to the blanket, but kept her eyes on the heaving water, unaware of the others.

As the swells rolled shoreward the volume increased until each wave crested, round and sparkling green at its height, then fell forward in a tumbling line of white foam that came to rest finally against the rocks farthest out in the sea. A ragged sheet of white bubbles rose high into the air.

One giant wave crested far out and they could see the dark shape of a sea lion in the milky-jade water. "What fun he's having surfing." Harry laughed and handed around cups of cider.

Jane leaned back on her elbows. "Did you ever try to imagine," she said, "what the coast would look like from a God's-eye view? The ragged shapes of North and South America sticking out into the ocean—the continents edged in white lace waves . . ."

Manuel took up the idea teasingly. "And all the Pacific Islands sticking out of the blue like raisins."

"I'm always reminded," said Harry, biting into a dough- nut, "when my kid sisters are gathering shells that every one of them was once the home of a live creature. That means that every cove on the millions of miles of ocean shore is the graveyard of a million years of sea life."

"Oh, Harry, don't be gloomy," murmured Jane.

"I don't think it's gloomy at all," he answered in surprise. "It's just fact."

"Kirsten has had a great idea," interrupted Manuel. "Jane, do you know what a *Baile de los Cascarones* is?"

"I do," said Harry. "My Dad has a *cascarón* that's sup- posed to be filled with real gold dust."

Jane's eyes glowed. "They're eggs, aren't they? Blown eggs filled with confetti."

"Yes, and they'd sure be a novelty at a dance," said Kir- sten rather uncertainly.

"Kirstie, how did you think of such a marv idea? You want us to have a dance for you?"

"Not for me, for Aunt Grace."

"Oh grand!"

Jane rolled over on her stomach and began to trace an M in the sand. "I bet that's the message the ghost has been trying to bring you," she said, but her voice was serious, not teasing.

Kirsten brought them up to date then about the recent noises in Stevenson House. Harry leaned forward.

"Your aunt should have gone across the porch and broken in on the ghost," he said. "Whoever is doing these things would surely have been right in the next room."

Kirsten shook the remains of the sugar from the doughnut bag into her hand, and licked her fingers thoughtfully. "She did just that—in spite of me! I was afraid it might be a man with murderous ideas. But Aunt Grace looked through all the rooms upstairs and didn't find anyone or anything."

"I don't blame you for being scared," shivered Jane.

"She should have phoned the police again," said Harry.

"She did next morning, but they didn't find anything either. She'd done all she could that night, and she's a little tired of always getting them over there on a wild-goose chase."

"Come on, we can't solve your aunt's problems now. The tide's out—it's time to explore the tide pools. Follow me, Kirsten. You guys coming?" Harry looked at Jane and Manuel.

Manuel shook his head. "Maybe later."

Kirsten was glad she had worn her old sneakers; they gripped the rough rocks as she followed Harry over the jagged course. He did not look around nor take her arm as Roger would have done. He simply assumed that she was as interested as he was in the things he could show her. The receding tide had left pools in the crevices between the big granite boulders. From the side the pools were like mirrors reflecting the sky, but looking down into them Harry and Kirsten could see a whole new world revealed through the crystal clearness.

94

Harry reached into the water and brought out a small snail shell. Holding it in his palm he whistled gently into the opening. A leggy creature popped out and backed in again at once. "Hermit crab," he explained. "They live in the shells of dead sea snails."

"How did you know one was in there?"

"Why, I saw it moving. Didn't you see it move!" Harry's voice held amazement, and Kirsten felt like a dull pupil. "Your eyes will get used to the rocks and the water and you'll soon see the life there."

Kirsten stared into the pool. Soon she could make out the same variety of metallic-brown kelp she had seen from the glass-bottomed boat.

"The harder you look the more you see," said Harry. The pebbles at the bottom of the pool began to move and they saw more hermit crabs carrying discarded snail shells on their backs. A few green-backed rock crabs ventured out from the crevices above the water and scampered sidewise over the rocks with their pink claws held aloft.

Kirsten, reaching down for a pearly saucer of abalone shell, watched her arm shrinking to half its length. "Distortion from refraction," said Harry, smiling.

Bright scarlet sponges and dark-green sea anemones, with rosettes of waving pink tentacles, held fast to the rocks. Dropping a pebble on one of the anemones, Kirsten watched it close instantly. "It's an animal, not a flower," said Harry.

"Life and death," said Kirsten, remembering what he had said about sea shells. "Oh, Harry, I never dreamed when I left home this June that there was so much I didn't know."

10

When Kirsten thought of Roger during this time it was usually at night, in an unhappy mood. His last letter had contained two sentences she must acknowledge, and she was afraid a frank answer would only widen the rift that was growing between her and Roger. Over and over she reread the sentences, "Once when Lorna was baby-sitting for your folks I stayed with her till they came back, and I must admit we had such fun dancing I didn't really mind that you were gone. . . . The job isn't much and sometimes I think I will just chuck it and join the navy."

She knew that she was jealous of Lorna, who had always been prettier than she was and had delighted in getting all the dates that might otherwise have been Kirsten's. But now, in addition to her anger at Lorna, she experienced her own share of guilt. Finally she wrote Roger a long letter, telling him all about her recent good times with Manuel,

Jane, and Harry. Her conscience troubled her slightly as she realized that she was trying to make him jealous too. But was the sourness of jealousy all that was left of love? She was vaguely relieved that Roger considered joining the navy. This would surely postpone their marriage, unless he hoped for a hasty wedding before he enlisted!

Kirsten ended her letter with only an oblique reference to Roger's: "Tell Lorna I don't mind your enjoying dancing with her. But I do mind your talk about going into the navy—unless that's what you really want."

She hoped to communicate to him some of her feelings about the beauties of the ocean and the wind-swept shores. But after staring vacantly into the magnolia tree she realized that Roger would probably be embarrassed by her intensity.

On an afternoon in late July, Manuel came to the apartment alone. Kirsten's heart beat fast when she opened the door to him. "Manuel, how nice!"

"Will you go walking with me till I have to go to work, Kirsten?" There was a strange urgency in Manuel's manner. "I want to talk to you."

"Why, of course." But now her gladness at seeing him was clouded by a vague uneasiness.

They walked down to the Pacific Building, once used as a hotel, a county courthouse, and a tavern. A fountain lined with Spanish tile was set in the outer wall around the enclosed garden. Four large magnolia trees surrounded a tiled, octagonal fountain in the center and a row of lemon trees grew beside a colonnade covered with wisteria blooms.

They dropped down onto a bench in the sunny patio. Suddenly Manuel was more ill at ease than Kirsten had ever seen him. "Kirsten—uh—I'm taking Jane to a dance in Carmel Valley this evening." He looked away across the garden, his brilliant eyes slitted against the bright light.

Kirsten felt utterly stricken. It was as though her heart had fallen away into space, leaving just a shell of a girl there on the bench. "Why should I care?" she wondered miserably. "I have Roger."

Manuel's fingers closed over hers. "It's—I told you long ago—I've had a case on Jane for as long as I can remember."

"I know." She gave a forlorn giggle. "I guess I thought I could charm you away from her."

His fingers pressed hers, then he took her hand in both his own and held it tightly while he gazed into space. She snatched it away.

"Don't you feel sorry for me," she cried.

"Why do you mind, when you have your own boy friend?"

"He's not a boy friend," she said hotly. "He's my fiancé, and don't you forget it."

"Don't you forget it either," he said gently.

Nervously turning her diamond ring she spoke quickly. "It's just that I long so for an evening date—dancing, not daytime stuff. Eating and swimming and yakking."

"I know." His voice was low. "Dancing is different. But I did finally have to decide, you know. Between you, that is."

Her bitterness was sharp. "Guess that wasn't hard."

His own voice was troubled. "A little. I do like you, Kirsten. You have qualities Jane doesn't have."

She would not be consoled. "Go ahead, say it—I'm quaint."

"No, you're different. Serious. Maybe old for your years. And nice. That's why I've said I wish you were my sister."

As they walked back to Stevenson House Manuel brought up the *Baile de los Cascarones*. "Jane and I were talking about it."

Kirsten's answer was cold. "I don't know when you and Jane have so much time to talk about things."

"Well—I phoned her to ask her to this dance."

"And she didn't tell me." Kirsten felt betrayed.

"Oh, Kirsten, you should know—you've been around."

"I guess it always hurts when someone else is preferred."

"It does. I know."

99

After a minute Kirsten forced a laugh. "About that ball. It would be fun, I should think, for you and Jane. Why don't you go ahead and plan it?"

"Kirsten, be reasonable. It's something *you* thought of for your aunt, you know. You could go with Harry."

"Harry?" Her voice went high in surprise.

"Well sure. What's wrong with him?"

"Two things. He doesn't care about me. And he does care about Jane."

"You make a big thing about love. People don't fall in love just because they go to high school dances together for four years. People fall into and out of love. There are many yardsticks, not just the one you measure yourself and Roger against."

She was miserable. Manuel went on, "If I asked Jane to ask him to ask you . . ."

Kirsten turned away from him abruptly. "I don't want to talk about it. Just leave Harry out of this."

Manuel spoke softly as he came over and took her arm. "Kirsten, for an engaged girl you do act sort of funny."

She felt the tears sting her eyes. "Oh, I wish I knew what Roger was doing right this minute," she said.

They separated at the corner. Manuel went on to work and Kirsten walked alone to the museum. Her aunt looked up from the reception desk, and Kirsten saw that Grace was upset.

"Look at this. Someone found it in the Stevenson bedroom and brought it down to me just now." She held out a sheet of paper on which appeared, in pale lavender ink, the words, "Each month I come back in the dark of the moon. R.L.S." They were written in a round sloping backhand.

Grace's color was high with anger. "This is really going too far," she said. "Whoever thinks he can play this silly game indefinitely is due for a shock."

Kirsten sat beside her aunt, holding the paper and staring at it. "What more can you do? Call the police again?"

Grace flung out her hands and the people-counter rolled

100

across the floor. While Kirsten retrieved it for her, Grace spoke rapidly. "It could be someone who worked here once. I had to discharge a janitor in April."

"You never told me that."

"I hadn't thought of him before. He could have had my keys duplicated. It could even be any one of your friends."

"Harry? Manuel? Jane?" Kirsten almost shouted and at a gesture from her aunt lowered her voice. There were still visitors in the rooms. "You might as well suspect one of the policemen."

"Kirsten, I've suspected everyone," said Grace in great distress. "Everyone but you and me."

"Well, I can assure you," began Kirsten angrily, then checked herself. Just because her own life seemed to be falling to pieces, she need not take out her disappointment on her aunt. "We'll find out who's making all this trouble," she said. "I haven't helped you much up to now, Aunt Grace, but I will." It would be good to turn her attention away from boys who caused her nothing but misery anyway.

Kirsten was glad that she had been asked to baby-sit for the Weidmans that evening. But all the time she read to the two little boys, and later watched television, she kept thinking of Jane and Manuel.

If she had thought Jane would sleep late the next morning she found herself mistaken. Her friend was at Stevenson House earlier than ever, eager to tell all about the wonderful time she had had with Manuel.

"He's a perfectly heavenly dancer," Jane said. "I never knew how much fun dancing could be. And he likes you, Kirstie," she added generously. "We talked about the *Baile de los Cascarones* you're planning for your aunt. He thinks it's a great idea. You know how he loves anything tied up with history. You could work it through Max Weidman, I should think. Let's talk to him real soon. He knows all the big shots around here, Chamber of Commerce and so on. We might talk him into planning a dance on a big scale, a kind of city party like Monterey used to have. That's Manuel's hope. Think big. In high school they used to call me 'the girl who thinks big.' "

Suddenly Kirsten was angry, and she felt justified in her anger. She could not hold it against Jane that Manuel had asked her to a dance, but she could and did object to having even her ideas taken away from her.

"Just a minute, Jane," she said firmly. "This was my idea, and I never intended a dance—on a big scale—as you call it. A city party! No thanks! Just friends of Aunt Grace. Think big if you want to, but I want this to be perfect. It's the only thing I can think of that would half repay my aunt for asking me out here for a whole summer."

Jane had taken out her knitting and was working quickly with her head bent low over the pink wool. When she spoke her voice was unusually humble. "Of course, Kirstie. I'm sorry."

Kirsten brightened at once, pleased with herself for having been strong enough to stand up to Jane. "I think it would be fun to go in costumes and masks," she said quickly. "We might be able to borrow some old clothes from the museums. What do you think?"

"That would be really fun," said Jane, happy again. "Come on, let's wash our hair. I hope you bought the shampoo."

"I forgot. We'll have to go over to the store for it."

Jane shook her head. "I wouldn't dare. Harry's mad at me. He asked me out last night and I went out with Manuel instead."

"Okay, you read the paper till I get back." Kirsten looked for Harry when she had found the shampoo in the store. He was at the farthest check-out counter. Luckily no one was in line there. She went over and waited for him to ring up her purchase.

"Hi, Kirstie," he said, counting out the change into her hand. "I meant to call you this morning, see if you were busy tonight. I've got tickets for the melodrama at the First Theater. You haven't been there yet, have you?"

Kirsten looked at him levelly. She wanted to say, "Why

don't you ask Jane? You know I'm engaged to a boy back home." But a date was a date.

"I'll ask Aunt Grace," she said. "She's not keen on my going out at night. Our garden is so spooky, and I think she's a little afraid of being in that old house alone."

"Well, there's no danger to you in a garden lighted like a Christmas tree. Maybe you just don't want to go with me."

"I'd like to go, really." She knew what it was like to feel rejected. "I'll call you back when my aunt comes up at noon. Unless you don't want to wait that long. Maybe you'd better ask Jane." She could not resist this.

"I'm asking you," he said stubbornly.

"Okay. I'll call you."

Kirsten crossed Munras Avenue absent-mindedly. She walked slowly along the path, between bushes of fragrant Scotch broom full of talkative bees. She decided not to tell Jane that Harry had asked her out.

By the time they had washed Kirsten's hair and put it up on rollers she had forgiven her friend. But she still had not said a word about Harry. Then Jane washed her own hair and brushed it in the sun on the upstairs porch. Kirsten saw how it caught the sunlight and shone like precious metal. She would have given her soul to be blond.

Kirsten was uneasy about her first date in Monterey. She felt guilty because of Roger and tried to quiet her conscience by being critical of Harry.

But there was really nothing to criticize. He was at ease with her aunt, rising when she entered the room, making conversation about everything from the ghost of Stevenson House to the price of hamburgers. He had even cleaned his old car for the evening.

The First Theater had once been a private house. Made of adobe, it had a handsome front porch of hand-hewn beams and a lobby decorated in the style of an early saloon. The floor boards were worn hollow in places from the steps of thousands of visitors. In the light of hanging lamps they gave up their tickets and were shown to a long rough bench in the center of the small hall.

Kirsten entered delightedly into the spirit of the play. Along with Harry she extravagantly cheered the handsome hero. She groaned when the heroine was in her deepest trouble, and she hissed the villain with vigor and enthusiasm.

Between the acts a young woman played an old upright piano as the audience shouted out the titles of old songs. Kirsten knew most of the words, and Harry looked at her in admiration while he mumbled occasional words in a monotone.

After the play came an olio, when all the cast members performed vaudeville acts and sang ridiculous songs. At the curtain call Kirsten stared at one very large man in a Little Lord Fauntleroy suit, then looked at her program and exclaimed, "Why, it's Max Weidman! And he was Colonel Rycroft in the play. What a change! Big as he is I didn't recognize him."

"Max is a regular old pro," said Harry. "His wife used to be an actress before she had the children. Come on, I'll give you a choice—either sand dabs and french fries, or chocolate sodas at Hermann's."

"Sand dabs! Whatever are they?"

"They're the best eating little fish on the West Coast."

"Let's have them then, by all means."

When at midnight they left his car at the curb outside Stevenson House, they walked through the garden and up the stairs in silence. "Let's sit on the step a minute and talk," said Harry.

They could smell the latest magnolia flower flaunting its sweetness in the moonlight. "White flowers smell sweetest at night," said Harry, "to attract the moths."

Kirsten's laugh was soft and teasing. "For goodness' sake, don't take the romance out of things by explaining them." But that was like Harry, she reflected later. He was as literal as cold water and as real as good bread.

11

Kirsten hurried through the dishes and was dressed when Jane arrived the next morning. "I just saw Max Weidman downstairs," said Jane breathlessly. "Let's go down and talk to him about—"

Kirsten put her finger to her lips. "Sh-h." She nodded toward her aunt's room. "It's got to be a secret."

Grace came out then in a bright-blue suit that matched the blue of her eyes. She had combed her black hair trimly into a pompadour, with a french roll at the back. She gathered up notebooks, pen, and purse from the table, saying, "Good morning, Jane. 'Bye, dear, I'll be home for lunch."

Kirsten followed her to the door and wistfully watched her go down the steps to the patio. "How smart she looks," she thought. "There must be some secret. Here she is, middle-aged—forty this month. Why can't I dress like that?"

She turned back to Jane, who was humming happily and practicing a dance step. "Come on, now," she said. "Let's ask Mr. Weidman to help us make a list of Aunt Grace's friends. He's known her for years. I'm sure he'd know most of them. Also I've got to decide where we can have the dance, but I can't till I know how many to ask."

Max looked up as they came into the reception room downstairs. Kirsten could still see traces of mascara around his bright eyes. "You made a wonderful Colonel Rycroft in the play last night," she said.

"Thank you, Kirsten."

She sensed Jane's surprise and looked at her with some triumph. "I went with Harry," she replied to the unasked question.

"That was our first performance," said Max. "We're doing the same play again tonight and next weekend. My wife and I were wondering if you'd like to be top girl on our baby-sitter list, Kirsten?"

"Oh my, yes. I'm running out of spending money. And I need some now for a special purpose." Kirsten talked excitedly. "That day Aunt Grace and I came to the Custom House I saw a display of *cascarones,* and I got a brainstorm. I thought what fun it would be to have a dance using them the way they used to in the old days in Monterey. I want to do something special for Aunt Grace, she's done so much for me. Jane and I thought you could tell us the names of all her friends. We could find their addresses in the phone book and send them invitations. But we'd have to hire a hall, I guess. And that would take money."

Max's eyes were sparkling with enthusiasm. "Grace has made a lot of friends since she came here ten years ago," he said. "It would take the armory to give a party for her."

Kirsten puffed out her cheeks in vexation. "Sounds like more money than I could save up," she said. "We've only got a month."

"I think we could get the armory for twenty dollars if

we choose a week night. It's always busy on weekends and the price is at least double. Then an orchestra . . ."

Kirsten looked bleak. "That would cost so much money. I couldn't—" she began, but Max interrupted.

"Let me ask the members of the Actors' Guild," he said. "That woman who plays the piano at the First Theater belongs to a combo. All old friends of Grace's too."

Kirsten expressed her relief by dropping like a rag doll into a chair beside the desk. "We'd still have to pay them."

"Probably not, Kirsten. Maybe some little gift to each."

"Oh that would be fun," cried Jane. "If you'll let me, Kirstie, I'll help you find something."

"Doesn't have to be much," said Max. "A box of notepaper or ear rings—costume jewelry is something all performers love."

Never before had Kirsten felt so certain of herself. "We'll do it," she said, "with your help, Mr. Weidman. I feel as though I should baby-sit for nothing."

"No, indeed, we have to pay someone. And our boys have never been so enthusiastic before about a baby-sitter. Apparently you have some special skill with children."

Kirsten was inordinately pleased. "It's because I have so many brothers and sisters, I guess. I only wish Louis Castro would play with your boys."

"So do I, but all he seems to want to do is go it alone or follow Manuel around."

"We'll have to blow an awful lot of eggs—and dye them," said Jane thoughtfully. "And fill them with confetti. Harry says his father has a *cascarón* filled with gold dust. Maybe he'd give us that."

"Not likely," Max laughed. "That's pretty valuable."

"Another thing," said Kirsten. "I'd like it to be a costume affair. Do you suppose we might borrow some clothes from the museums?"

"I think we could. But how could you get your aunt to dress up without telling her?"

"Gosh!" Kirsten leaned her elbows on the desk. She thought aloud slowly. "Harry will come by and ask me to go for a ride—he wants to show me something—"

"And we'll have a costume ready for her in the powder room at the armory," interrupted Jane. "I know your aunt's size, and I'll just bet she could wear that embroidered velvet dress you have on display at the Custom House, Mr. Weidman. You know that one that was made for a bride who came from New Orleans way back in 1849."

Max nodded. Kirsten had the feeling that this was going to be as much fun for him as it was for the girls. "It would be as good as play-acting," she reminded him.

"It will be fun," he agreed, changing her verb to a positive mood. He looked teasingly at Jane. "But we'll have to revive the old dances," he said. "Waltzes and fox-trots, even the two-step. None of this modern oddball stuff."

"Don't call it oddball," warned Jane, laughing. "I like the modern dances. They really make you feel you're shrugging off the cares of the world."

"You might be able to learn something really pretty and graceful like a waltz."

"If it's dancing I could learn it."

Kirsten was dreaming again. "Maybe we could get some of my aunt's friends to serenade the way they used to in Stevenson's day—roaming the streets, you know. I read about it in one of his essays. Sometimes they went alone, sometimes in groups with guitars."

"She'd like that, Kirsten." Max spoke appreciatively.

But next morning there was new trouble at the museum. Max Weidman came up to the apartment while Grace and Kirsten were still eating breakfast.

"Have a cup of coffee?" asked Grace.

"Thanks, I will." He stirred sugar and cream into his cup and sat looking troubled. "Grace, I'm missing the key to the trunk room door from my key ring. I wondered if you might have found it."

She shook her head. "When did you notice it was gone?"

"When I set the burglar alarm last night. I tried the door and it was unlocked, so I set the alarm. But then I couldn't lock up afterwards because my key wasn't on the ring. I should have told you at once, but I was in a hurry."

"Maybe the key fell off the ring, or maybe one of your boys took it off."

"Could be. Kids do things for the unlikeliest reasons. But the oddest thing is that when I passed the trunk room just now I tried the door and found it locked. Did you lock it?"

"No, I didn't."

"Well, someone now has that key of mine and can go in there whenever he likes. And all your research files are in there, as well as the trunks."

"Let's go down and see if anything is missing."

Kirsten, more pleased by the excitement than she would have admitted, went down with them.

"The files are all locked and won't open except to this key," said Grace. "They look all right, so there's no use checking them. But let's see if anything's missing from the trunks. Some valuable old clothes have come in lately and I'd planned to change the exhibits in the sewing room and the bedrooms soon."

Grace walked over to the corner near the small window. "Well, look here!" Kirsten and Max followed her. She shook out a heap of clothes untidily bundled together: two dark square *mantas*, a brown wadmal coat, and several old woollen dresses.

"Now who in the world . . ."

None of them could think of an answer to that. One after another Grace opened the trunks and went through them. Over the contents of the third trunk Kirsten gasped in delight.

Her aunt drew out a toreador's suit of fine black wool—pants, bolero, and flat black hat. All were trimmed in silver: buckles, braid curling into frogs, and buttons tarnished now by time but silver nevertheless. There were even black high-heeled shoes and round silver spurs.

Grace shook out two blouses, one low-necked and short-sleeved, the other with turned-down collar and ballooning full sleeves. There were also a black lace mantilla, a pair of castanets, a red-flowered skirt, and a carved tortoise-shell comb.

"There's nothing missing," said Grace. "Nothing wrong except those clothes in the corner. I wonder who put them there. Now I'll have to get padlocks for the trunks."

On the following Wednesday Grace decided to stay at home all morning, and Kirsten was frantic. She had intended to talk to Max Weidman about plans for the ball, but she did not dare to go down to see him while her aunt was there.

Jane did not arrive until almost eleven. "I had to give Mama a shampoo and set," she explained. "She wants it in the morning so she'll have all day for it to dry. Do you want to go shopping? I need some new stockings and I've saved enough to buy Mama a record. She likes gospel songs."

"All right with you, Aunt Grace?"

"Yes, yes, go along. I'm going to type my article for the historical society magazine."

As they ran downstairs Kirsten said, "Let's stop and talk to Max about the dance. I want to see how he's coming with the plans."

Max was at the desk, and his sons, Jock and Harold, were on the floor coloring pictures in a large book. Louis Castro was sitting in a corner peeling the wrapper from a purple crayon. Kirsten went over to give him a quick hug but he shrank back, glancing at the other boys with embarrassed eyes.

"How's plans, Mr. Weidman?" Jane leaned on the desk.

Max produced a list of several pages of names. "Well, it will certainly take the armory for all Grace's friends," he said. "My wife helped me make out the list. They're mostly curators in the State buildings and members of the Actors' Guild. Your father insisted he must be there to honor Grace even though your mother can't come. And there are a dozen

rich old ladies from Pebble Beach and Carmel and around the Seventeen Mile Drive—people who have been in contact with Grace about gifts to Stevenson House. I didn't know Grace had so many friends."

Kirsten had never planned nor yet carried out a social affair of any proportion greater than a Camp Fire Girls' ceremonial meeting. Now suddenly she was involved in intense and secret preparations for a party more important than any she had ever attended.

"It might almost as well be my wedding," she thought once.

Again and again she and Jane wrote on heavy deckle-edged linen, "Please come to a Masquerade Ball at the Armory in Monterey on the night of August 30. . . ." When they had finished, there were thirty-five couples, which meant seventy people invited to the party. They had given Jane's home address, and from day to day she brought the replies for Kirsten to check off against a master list. Apparently everyone planned to attend.

Their secret meetings with Max Weidman were constantly interrupted by Aunt Grace's unannounced entrances. Kirsten was sure she would begin to suspect something, but her aunt was too involved in the mystery of the ghost. And so the plans for the party shaped up and became the scaffolding of reality. The pianist for the First Theater, Edna Gould, entered whole-heartedly into the plan. Her musical group agreed to play for the party without charge. The armory manager gave Kirsten a receipt in payment for an evening's rent, dated August 30. Kirsten worked off her debt by baby-sitting for the Weidmans at the rate of seventy-five cents an hour. On several weekends the Weidmans were away from home all day Saturday and Sunday, and her earnings mounted up.

"Whatever are you going to do with all your money?" asked her aunt one evening.

"Oh, I'll find something worth spending it on," said Kirsten.

Max had obtained permission from the local head of the State Division of Beaches and Parks to use the costumes in the museums in Monterey. And one after another wives and husbands were outfitting themselves in the costumes of the old Spanish capital. Kirsten longed to borrow the Spanish costumes she had seen in the Stevenson House trunk room, and one day determined on a way to ask her aunt without arousing her suspicions.

"Do you think the Actors' Guild could borrow those old costumes in the trunk room for a play, Aunt Grace?"

"Possibly," her aunt replied. "All they need to do is ask me."

Kirsten reported this to Max and he promised that he would ask Grace for them.

Meantime there were all the *cascarones* to make. Unknown to Grace, the word was spreading among all her friends: Save whole eggshells! Make a hole at both ends of an egg with a pin, then enlarge the holes to about one-eighth of an inch and blow out the contents. Then bring the shells to the home of Jane Tinsley.

Day after day, Jane and Kirsten washed and dried the shells, then dyed them in many colors. Lastly they pasted a bit of colored paper over one end and filled the shells with colored confetti. They pasted another bit of paper over the other end and, behold—a genuine *cascarón*! Never had Kirsten experienced so much pleasure in accomplishment.

And at last she met Jane's mother. Jane took her friend into the bedroom where lay a little woman with the most delicate skin and the smallest face Kirsten had ever seen. Mrs. Tinsley reached out a thin hand that felt as cool as ivory. Her smile was the sweetest thing the girl could imagine.

"Jane has told me so much about you. Now finally we meet."

"I know now why Jane is such a nice girl."

"Thank you, dear." The voice was so weak that Kirsten

backed out of the room almost guiltily. But later Jane told her, with tears in her eyes, "You're the only one of my friends Mama has ever met. She doesn't like people to see her lying there. She used to be so active. You're good for people, Kirstie."

Kirsten felt a surge of happiness that lasted all the afternoon, as the girls worked together in the Tinsley kitchen. It was a happy sunny place, full of the sound of Mrs. Tinsley's bright-orange canary.

They had managed to color and fill *cascarones* until they had made six dozen. They let their fancy roam and Kirsten realized that given time she might develop a real skill at painting small scenes on the rounded sides of eggs. They wrapped the delicate objects in cotton batting and packed them in cartons.

"What's this new thing about your going to Jane's house every afternoon?" asked Grace one evening.

"Oh-h—she introduced me to her mother one day—and it turns out her mother really likes me."

"You have a way with people, dear."

"Thank you, Aunt Grace."

"I hope you're having enough fun here. It seems to me you've been awfully quiet lately."

"Lots of fun, thank you." Kirsten spoke eagerly, wishing she could tell her aunt about the dance. But it would be much more fun to surprise her.

"Is everything all right between you and Roger?"

Kirsten's heart thudded. "Well—yes. Why do you ask?"

"I only wondered. You seldom mention him."

Later that evening when she was alone in her bedroom, Kirsten reflected on her conversation with her aunt. She turned her ring so that the diamond faced her palm. But that made the gold band look too much like a wedding ring.

Too much like a wedding ring! "Yes," finally she had to admit it to herself, "I don't want to marry yet." The thought was so overpowering, so complete and definite, that it shocked her. She wondered how she could have thought herself ready for such an important step as accepting the love of a husband, a partner for life. "I'm more interested in plans for the ball than I've ever been in a wedding," she admitted bleakly. "What was I thinking of? Just someone to emphasize me and my importance. Oh, Roger, I would have wronged you if I had married you feeling that way."

Actually she spent many of her waking hours wondering if she would have a date to the masked ball. When she and Jane had made the *cascarones* they had expected that Manuel and Jane would make one couple, Kirsten and Harry another. But suppose Harry did not ask her to go? Would she swallow her pride and ask him instead?

Jane telephoned one afternoon. "Oh, Kirstie, I couldn't wait to call you. Manuel just asked me to the ball. Isn't it wonderful! I think I'm in love. I really do!"

"Oh, please, Jane!" Kirsten's voice squeaked. "Please don't fall in love just when I'm beginning—"

"I've got to dash back to Mama now," interrupted Jane. "She's waiting for me to read to her. She's got one of her headaches, but I had to let you know."

"That's great, Jane."

Kirsten had been sustained for many days by the knowledge that a new dimension was shaping her life. She was admitting finally that at seventeen she had not arrived at all the answers. She had tried to settle for an easy solution of her future, and boredom would surely have been the outcome. Perhaps life was just beginning!

When the end of the day came and Harry had not telephoned her, Kirsten went to bed early. "Why should he hurry?" she thought miserably. "He knows no one else will ask me. He can take his own time about it, or not ask me at all."

She tried to read but nothing appealed to her. She lay in bed, looking out at the magnolia tree, but all she could think of was Harry's remark, "White flowers smell best at night to attract the moths." It was apparently easier for white flowers to attract moths than for her to attract boys.

She did not intend to start daydreaming about Harry, a boy who had at least seven years of schooling ahead before he could think of getting married.

"Good heavens," she said aloud, "where did the idea of Harry's getting married come from? Don't I have enough trouble trying to see ahead for myself and Roger? What kind of no-goodnik am I anyway?"

She turned on her light and resolutely looked for something unromantic to read. She would try some kid stuff. She opened *A Child's Garden of Verses* at random and read:

> It is the season now to go
> About the country high and low,
> Among the lilacs hand in hand,
> And two by two in fairy land.
>
> And he to her a hero is
> And sweeter she than primroses;
> Their common silence dearer far
> Than nightingale or mavis are.

Kirsten closed the book with a bang and turned out her light.

12

For several days Kirsten avoided the store where Harry worked, shopping instead at the market farther down the street. Jane came over every morning to talk about the costume she was making. "I'm going as Empress Eugénie, in apricot satin. It will be dreamy with my green eyes and yellow hair, don't you think? Manuel says he likes green eyes—especially mine."

Kirsten was sick of hearing about Manuel. When the talk turned to him, she usually suggested a walk.

"I wish Harry would ask you," said Jane. "I saw him yesterday evening, cutting the lawn, and I even suggested that he ask you so we could double-date. He just didn't answer. I guess he's got a right to be mad at me for dating Manuel. After all we'd gone steady most of our high school years. But he needn't be sulky. You're sulky too this morning."

"Oh, Jane, stop chattering."

That afternoon to give her spirits a lift, Kirsten decided to bake cookies. She would make enough to fill all the coffee cans. But first she would have to buy supplies at the supermarket.

Sauntering slowly down the aisles between the shelves, getting all the things she needed, Kirsten pretended not to see Harry at the check-out counter. She even went to another checker with her cart. Then she hefted the brown bag of groceries and started toward the door.

"Kirsten! Wait a minute."

Harry called to another clerk, who was unpacking a crate of lettuce, "Take my counter, Jim. I'll be right back."

Harry took her groceries and walked with her out to the curb. "Kirsten, what's wrong? You haven't been in the store for days."

She looked down at her feet. "You could have phoned me."

"Well, I wondered. I didn't want to crowd you."

"Crowd me?"

"I talked to my dad about you last Sunday. He said if I . . ." Harry bit his lower lip and hesitated so long that Kirsten looked into his face.

"If you what?"

"He said if I really like you I'd better take it slow because you're only out here for the summer and you've got a boy friend back home. He never did like my going steady with Jane. He said it's a mistake in school. People get ideas and go in over their heads. And I've got a lot of hard work ahead of me before I can get serious about a girl."

She said nothing until he asked urgently, "Kirstie?"

She laughed softly. "Well, you can't be *too* practical. I guess you have to take some chances. I won't get involved if you don't."

"It's not that I don't want to, Kirsten. But my folks are going to help me through college, and I can't let them down. I've gotta take it slow and easy. And you . . ."

"I've got a lot of thinking to do," she said quietly. "About you, about Manuel, about Roger. I guess I was younger than I thought I was when I came out here in June."

"Kirstie—"

"Yes?"

"I know I'm not a good dancer, but I'd sure appreciate it if you'd go to the masked ball with me."

She hoped she would not begin to skip on her way home. Sometimes, even at seventeen, when she was suddenly happy, she skipped.

On the next day came the letter Kirsten had been dreading. It was a relief to hold it in her hands, though they were shaking. She read:

Dear Kirsten,

It looks to me like I made a mistake in you. I thought you were one girl I could trust but you're no better than my mother. When she two-timed my dad that was the end.

We had such good times last year I can hardly believe you've changed so toward me. I can read between the lines as well as the next one. You needn't spell it out that you've fallen for another guy.

I got so upset when I got your letter that I got a ticket for speeding. Now my dad won't let me drive except to work and back. Don't be surprised if my next letter is from San Diego. I still think I may go into the Navy. Dave Loudermilk wants me to enlist with him. He and Janet have broken up.

I really love you, Kirsten, and I'll give you a chance to come back and be like you were last spring. Better be good. Keep wearing my ring and I'll see you in a month now.

Yours ever,
Roger

Kirsten read the letter through several times. "He loves me, he loves me not. What do I do now?"

She decided to put love out of her mind for a while. She laid Roger's ring with his letters in her top bureau drawer. She did not feel right about wearing it until she saw him again.

She waited impatiently, day after day, for Max Weidman

to borrow the Spanish costumes. Then perhaps she and Harry could wear them to the ball. She told Harry about them and tried to persuade him so that he should wear the toreador suit.

"That would look better on Manuel," he said. "After all, he's part Spanish. You can't make me over, Kirstie."

"I don't want to," she replied quickly. She had a more pressing problem to think about anyway; she was not a good dancer.

"You should take lessons," Jane said one morning as they were walking on Alvarado Street. "There's a good dancing school down the street here. You could sign up for some lessons or you could practice with me in your aunt's apartment. She has some good records and I can bring some of mine."

"Well, I'd rather have you show me. I'd die of mortification if I had to take dancing lessons."

Jane laughed. "Okay, I need practice myself in those old-fashioned waltzes. I always start to do the two-step. They're so much alike, but a waltz is ever so much more dippy and glidy and graceful."

"I hope Harry knows how to dance."

"He's not so bad. I think he'll do better on the old-fashioned dances than he does with rock 'n' roll. He's got a certain amount of grace. Nothing like Manuel, of course. Harry never had time to go to dances, except for the big school dance at the end of the year. Papa liked Harry because he wasn't what Papa called a 'lounge lizard.' "

"What an expression!"

"Yes, my parents must have been real weirdos. Let's go back and start the lessons now, Kirstie."

Jane was a born dancer. Though she kept protesting, "I'll ruin myself if I get into the habit of leading," Kirsten knew that she was not seriously worried, for Jane danced without effort. She was music itself, without body, without self-awareness.

Kirsten loved the specialty dances—the Mexican Hat Dance and the *Cueca* of Chile. "Manuel can do this beautifully," said Jane, demonstrating the fast courting step. "It's supposed to be the cock wooing the hen." She spoke breathlessly, snapping a handkerchief over her head and stamping her feet. "Being the cock, I'm supposed to have spurs on. Papa watched us last night and said it was better than all the frugging. You never can tell what old people will like."

"I do hope Mr. Weidman will ask Aunt Grace for those costumes soon," said Kirsten. "He's going to pretend that they're for a play at the First Theater, then lend them to Harry and me for the ball."

Then at noon, a day or so later, her aunt said, "Kirsten, Max wants to borrow those costumes you admired so much. If I get them out of the trunk will you see to it that the buttons are sewed tightly and all the rips are mended? They're pretty old."

"I'd be glad to," said Kirsten, hugging her elbows in secret excitement.

After supper they went to the trunk room.

"Kirsten, look!" Grace exclaimed, pointing to a pile of clothes, wadded up on the floor.

"But they can't be out of the trunks," Kirsten said in a puzzled voice. "They can't be! You put padlocks on all of them."

"No, they can't be, but they are."

Grace examined the trunks and found them still locked. "How in the world?" she gasped. Then she unlocked one of the trunks, and when she threw back the lid it flew against the wall and dropped to the floor.

"Aha!" she exclaimed, picking it up and examining the hinges at the back. "Someone unscrewed the hinges. The wood is so rotten you could take the screws out with your fingers."

Staring into the trunk, Kirsten gave a cry of dismay. "They're gone! They're gone!" she wailed, and began to tumble the contents of the trunk. There was nothing left except an old dark-red linsey-woolsey dress with rusty purple braid around the skirt and train, a black ostrich feather boa, and a bright green suit with shiny black braid trimming and puffed sleeves.

"Oh, Aunt Grace, the beautiful costumes, they're gone."

A faint noise outside the window caused Kirsten to look up. Her face froze while her heart thudded painfully. She grasped her aunt's arm with fingers strong and tense with fright.

"Aunt Grace—look! Look!"

A gaunt face stared in at them, a face neither one recognized. There was something inhuman about it, something that made Kirsten say breathlessly, "the ghost."

The face had a sweeping mustache and a little goatee. A lank lock of hair came down over the forehead, and bright dark eyes seemed to peer directly at Kirsten. She realized that the stranger could not see in. The trunk room was dusky with evening shadows, while the garden was filled with mellow light.

The figure cupped its hands against the pane, and pressed its face close to the glass. The moment that it saw the two women, it disappeared from sight. There was a rustle of bushes, but by the time Kirsten and Grace had run out the figure was gone.

"Oh, I don't like it," wailed Kirsten, "I thought it was such fun at first, a ghost here. But it's no fun at all."

"And it's no ghost either," said her aunt quietly. "That was a mask."

"Could you tell who it was?"

Her aunt did not answer for what seemed like minutes. Then she said in a whisper, "Those little grimy hands were a child's."

Grace looked out across the grounds, considering all the possible hiding places. Suddenly she grabbed Kirsten's arm and started for the tool shed at the other side of the museum.

"Come on," said Grace. "Maybe we'll finally catch our ghost."

Kirsten followed her at a run. Grace wrenched open the sagging door of the tool shed and there he was, cowering in a

corner, the mask held tightly in one small hand.

"Louis!"

"Louis Castro!"

He sank down on the floor, not taking his scared eyes from Grace's face.

Grace held his gaze like an avenging angel. "What were you doing in the garden, Louis?" she demanded.

"Just lookin'," he said sullenly.

"Have you been in that trunk room before?"

He nodded. "Couple nights I slep' there till Manuel came home. I don't like bein' all alone. When he goes out with Jane weekends, he's later than ever. It's no fun at home any more."

"But—all alone in that trunk room!"

"Well, this house is where *she* lives." He nodded toward Kirsten without looking at her. His voice was so low they could hardly hear the words.

Suddenly Grace extended her hand and took the mask. "Where did you get this?" she asked. "And why did you have it on?"

He rubbed his hands now as though they itched. Eleven years old—just the age of her brother Arnold, thought Kirsten. She could imagine Arnold planning tricks on his elders. But not like this!

"I got it at a store. All those actors get their masks and costumes there. Wigs 'n' things. It's supposed to be a poet mask."

"It looks like Robert Louis Stevenson," said Kirsten. Still he did not turn his eyes on her.

"I heard about the ghost here. I got the key for that room off Mr. Weidman's key ring one day when he left it on the desk a minute. Then I was downtown with his boys and I saw this mask. I thought it looked like the man in the picture—you know, the one that looks at you. So I took it."

"You mean you didn't pay for it?"

Louis shook his head warily as though afraid she would strike him. "I just thought I could put on some old clothes some night and scare you."

124

"Scare us?"

"I could pretend to be the ghost."

"But you're *not* the ghost?"

Louis shook his head vigorously. "How could you think that?"

Kirsten went over and shook his bare shoulder gently. "Louis, tell the truth. You did take those Spanish costumes. You *are* the ghost."

He did not look up from his small hands, which he kept rubbing together. "Yes, I took 'em. I thought you and Manuel could wear 'em to a dance sometime. Only now he's takin' out that old Jane."

"Don't you like Jane?"

"She's all right. But she never looked at me in her life. You did. The very first time, you looked at me. You even read me a poem about someone named Louis. Almost like it was me."

Kirsten felt tears prick her eyes. She was not surprised when her aunt said, "Louis, come upstairs with us. We were just going to have something to eat. Are you hungry?"

He nodded and stood up. "Come on, then."

He ate everything set before him—a plate of bacon and eggs, two slices of hot toast oozing butter, a cup of cocoa on which Grace floated two fat marshmallows, and unnumbered fresh cookies. When he finally sat back from the table he patted his stomach and grinned. "Guess I was hungry," he said.

"Doesn't Manuel see that you get fed?" demanded Grace.

"We always have food around if that's what you mean," murmured Louis defensively. "But Manuel works from four till twelve every day 'cept weekends. We have one big meal at noon. Otherwise I just pick up what I want. Bowl of cornflakes an' milk for supper usually. It's no fun eatin' alone."

"What about breakfast?"

"Who eats breakfast?"

"Most of us do." Kirsten thought of the silver egg cup and the vicar's egg and the happy hour with the morning paper. How could they all have ignored Louis for so long? Alone in that dreadful yellow house among the tall anise weeds.

She wanted to blame Jane. Did Jane ever think anything about Manuel except that he was a "divine dancer"? Still Kirsten knew that she had been no better.

And Aunt Grace. She had known Manuel and Louis for almost a year now. And Mr. Tinsley—where did the responsibility begin? She looked at the clock. It was only nine. Louis would be alone for three hours if he went home now. Could her brother Arnold sleep if he were all alone in an old house?

"Come on," said Grace, "Kirsten and I will walk home with you."

"You crazy, Mrs. Douglas? I been runnin' the streets for two years, ever since my Aunt Rhetta died."

"Running the streets? Why did you start doing that?"

"Oh, Uncle Pedro married again. Lives out in Castroville. Who wants to live there? Manuel and I want to go it alone."

"How does your uncle feel about this?"

"He wants us to live with him an' his wife. They both go to the priest an' beg him an' he comes to see Manuel, but Manuel says we can get along fine without relatives."

"All the same we'll see you home," said Grace firmly.

As they went through the garden, with its alternating lights and shadows, Kirsten had a feeling of anticlimax. She was no longer afraid of the ghost. All she feared was that they would discover too much about little Louis and Manuel that they would rather not know.

When they returned to the lighted apartment Grace stacked the dishes in the sink. "Poor little ghost," she sighed.

"Imagine his wanting to see Manuel and me dancing in those costumes." Kirsten's heart was tender. She did not want to think past Louis's kindly impulse. "After all, he wasn't stealing for himself."

"But the other things, Kirsten. We'll have to ask him about all of them after we've had a talk with his brother."

13

There was a most uncomfortable hour next morning with Grace and Kirsten, Manuel and Jane. Jane arrived first at the apartment, glowing with the news (for Kirsten's ears alone) that Manuel had given her his ring to wear. She drew out a chain from around her neck and showed Kirsten a signet ring with Manuel's initials in the center and his high school class name and numerals around the edge.

"I have to wear it hidden," said Jane. "Dad would have a fit if he knew. Manuel's got four years of college and at least two or three more before he could even teach in a junior college. And as for a wife and family . . ."

"Besides, there's Louis," said Kirsten.

"Well of course there's Louis." Jane looked annoyed. "You don't suppose Manuel is going to desert his brother, do you?"

"Hush, here's Aunt Grace."

Manuel knocked at the door just as Grace came into the room. He and Jane looked puzzled when the older woman sat down on the couch among them. "How nice you look, Manuel," said Grace.

He did look handsome in his new dark suit. Kirsten wondered just how far Jane's influence would extend. First he had stopped wearing the soiled jacket and jeans in favor of brown slacks and shirt. Then he had changed his hair style and cut off his beard. Next he would be giving up his beloved motorcycle and driving a big car.

"I want to talk to you," said Grace, holding Manuel with her eyes. "Kirsten, will you bring the coffee pot and some cups and saucers?"

"It's about Louis, isn't it?" said Manuel suddenly.

Kirsten distributed the cups of coffee and napkins and spoons, glad to be busy while her aunt took charge of the conversation.

"Yes, it's about Louis. Last night while you were at work he came here, intending to get into the trunk room. Kirsten and I saw him looking in while we were down there and he tried to run away. But we found him in the tool shed. Manuel, had you any idea your brother was the ghost of Stevenson House?"

Jane jumped so that she spilled coffee on her skirt. She mopped it up nervously. Manuel did not take his eyes off Grace.

"No, I didn't," he said unhappily. "Are you sure, Mrs. Douglas?"

"About as sure as I can be without talking more to him. He was afraid of me and didn't admit anything except that he had been sleeping here while you worked. He stole the trunk-room key from Max's key ring one day, and probably he's borrowed other keys too."

"I can't understand it," gasped Jane. "A little kid like that—"

"A lonely little kid," said Grace severely, "with a good imagination and not enough to occupy his time. Manuel, I think you should take your brother out to live with your aunt and uncle in Castroville."

Manuel put down his coffee cup and leaning forward rested his elbows on his knees and folded his hands. "I think you're right, Mrs. Douglas. Father Dolan has been after me to do that for a long time. I just put it off."

"Well a brother isn't something you can put off. I want to go out and see Louis some evening, but I want him to be with his aunt first, let her talk to him about things. If we find that he did take the things that are missing from the museum, I'll have to report it to the police. I'm the curator here, and that's my duty."

Kirsten had never seen Manuel's black eyes when they were not merry or flirtatious or at least teasing. Now she saw their deep sadness.

Lighting a cigarette Manuel said earnestly, "I should have let Uncle Pedro have him. I should never have tried to go it alone."

"You should both have lived with your uncle, I think. He wanted you and apparently his new wife is kind."

Manuel nodded. "It was just—I don't know—sort of rebellion. Aunt Rhetta was the one we really loved, but Uncle Pedro couldn't help it that she died. And he was never mean. But Castroville is so far out, away from everything."

"Everything! There's a home for you both and three good meals a day. And from the way Louis ate here last night that's more than he's been getting." Grace was still severe. "Out there he'd have someone to see he's clean and send him to church on Sunday."

Manuel stared into space and his mouth was grim. "My little brother a thief," he said in a low voice. He stood up. "I think I'll go see Father Dolan now, Mrs. Douglas. You coming along, Jane?"

Jane's answering glance was tear-filled. "I'll walk with you to the parish house," she said, "but I can't go in. I should be with Mama this morning. She was having terrible pains in her shoulder when I left." She smiled faintly at Kirsten.

"I'm reading her *The Amateur Emigrant*," she said. "Mama says she never knew Stevenson had been so human."

"Where is Louis now?" Kirsten asked.

"He was asleep when I left home."

"Home! What a home!" thought the girl.

Kirsten had forgotten that this was Harry's free morning. When an hour later he appeared at the door she could have hugged him in her relief. "Oh, Harry, we've had such a dreadful time," she cried. "Louis Castro is the ghost and Aunt Grace has just been scolding Manuel and he's promised to move Louis out to his uncle's in Castroville."

"Whoa up," said Harry soothingly. Then the full force of her words hit him. "Louis is the ghost! Little Louis?"

"The same. I don't understand it all myself, and I do feel so miserable and disappointed. I love that kid as if he were my brother."

Awkwardly Harry patted her shoulder. "Kirsten, I came to ask you to go fishing this morning. Now I think you need that more than ever. Fishing is awfully good for the soul, especially when you're troubled about something. Come on, change your clothes and let's go down to the pier."

As on their first fishing date they bought squid and fished from the very end of the pier, where Harry said his luck had always been best. This time the day was gray and overcast. When they cast out, their lines made arcs in the strong wind.

Once the sinkers had carried their lines deep, they sat one on either side of a piling and talked around it. "Tell me more about Louis, Kirsten. How did you find out he was the ghost? How did he do all those things around the museum?"

"We were down in the trunk room last night and he was looking in. He had on a strange mask, he told us afterward it was a poet mask. He thought he looked like that portrait of Stevenson that's opposite Aunt Grace's desk. Funny kind of fantasy."

"Not for a bookworm like Louis. What happened when you saw him?"

"We didn't know who he was in the mask and we ran out to catch him. He ran into the tool shed on the other side of the museum. Then it suddenly struck us both that he had been causing all the trouble around Stevenson House. He didn't admit it, but I'm sure now."

Kirsten leaned her head against the piling and closed her eyes. She was so tired, so tired of it all, and so despondent over Louis. A moment later she was on her feet, reeling in her line. "Got a bite," she said tensely. And she forgot the Castros until she had landed a foot-long bocaccio.

"Good girl." Harry watched her rebait the hook, smiling at her calmness. "Jane always panics at the baiting bit."

"Jane thinks it's feminine to do that."

"You don't have to worry about being feminine."

"I know." Kirsten was a little surprised by her calm acceptance of this fact. So short a time ago Roger had scolded, "Girls don't do that, Kid. Don't try to be different." And she had said contritely, "I'm not trying to be, I guess I just am."

Kirsten sat quietly looking out across the gray water, hardly conscious of her fishing line. She watched a sea gull swoop down to a bright-blue fishing boat far out in the bay.

"Harry, do you think we could help Manuel if he decides to move out to his uncle's?"

"Help him? Oh, you mean help with the moving. Gosh, Kirsten, I've seen the place where they live and they don't have more than they could carry out in two suitcases. It's hardly more than a rented room. Maybe a few dishes and kitchen things."

"Oh, poor Manuel, poor Louis!"

Harry spoke rather critically. "It's the way Manuel wanted it. And Louis always wanted what Manuel wanted. They'll be all right. Oh-oh, got a bite!"

When they returned to Stevenson House at noon, Manuel was standing at the door of the reception room talking to Grace. He greeted them both with quiet restraint.

"Hi, who gets the big fish?"

Harry smiled. "We thought Mrs. Douglas might like one. Would you care for the other?"

"I'm not too fond of bocaccio, but I'll take it out to Aunt Maria. Louis and I moved out there this morning."

"Then everything's all right, isn't it?" Kirsten spoke almost gaily.

Her aunt looked at her surprised. "It's not quite as simple as all that, child. I was just asking Manuel whether he had talked to Louis."

"Louis wants to talk to you both," interrupted Manuel. "The sooner the better. I gather he wants to get the whole thing off his chest. Aunt Maria suggested you come out tonight. She's going to make him take a nap this afternoon." Manuel smiled briefly. "Guess Louis never had an afternoon nap in his life."

"I could take you in my car," volunteered Harry.

Manuel smiled at Grace. "That would be better than my motorcycle. And I have to work tonight."

"Come about seven," suggested Grace. "Like Louis, I want to get this whole thing cleared up."

Kirsten joined them that evening as they drove out to Louis's new home. All around Castroville artichoke fields fanned away toward the smoke-gray Gabilan Mountains. The Castros lived close to an artichoke packing shed. Here, even at night, under unshaded light bulbs men and women sorted artichokes from field lugs and packed them tightly in market crates.

Harry brought his car to a stop close to the porch built out over bare beaten earth. "I didn't have time to tell you about their Aunt Maria," he said quickly as he helped them out of the car. "She has three boys by an earlier marriage."

There was no time to answer, for three little black-eyed boys, strangely alike in age and coloring, came running out on the porch, all in clean overalls. "Hi, Harry," shouted one. "Louis saw you drive up. He'll be glad to see you."

Louis was on a wicker couch in the front room, watching television. A woman rose from a deep chair near him and turned off the set, then advanced to meet Kirsten, holding out her hand. Maria Castro was slim and dark, with abundant wavy hair growing gray at the temples. There was sadness in the brilliant eyes and there were lines in the cheeks; but once she had had great beauty. Her teeth flashed in a smile of welcome.

"So this is Manuel's Jane," she said, clasping Kirsten's hands.

Kirsten knew she must be blushing. "No, Mrs. Castro, this is Kirsten MacDonald," said Harry. "She's Louis's best friend, and he wanted to see her. And this is her aunt, Mrs. Douglas, the museum curator."

Maria Castro bobbed shyly and respectfully.

"Where's Pedro?" asked Harry, looking around.

"He's back on the night shift. It's hard on the boys because they have to be quiet while he sleeps all morning. But they're good boys," she added. "I'll get some lemonade. Sit down."

Louis rolled his black eyes toward his visitors, then away. He smiled shyly down at the floor, pursing his full lips. Kirsten felt her heart bursting with relief. At last they would know the truth.

"Hi," said Louis quietly.

Maria Castro came back with a tray of lemonade and cookies. "I'll keep the boys out," she said. "I know you want to talk with Louis."

Harry jerked his head toward the door when she had gone out. "She's wise," he said. "I don't know why Manuel held out against her for so long. Louis would have been better off living here all the time, even if she does have three other boys."

"Those boys will be good for Louis," said Kirsten. "Won't they, honey?" She turned her eyes on Louis and he nodded doubtfully.

Kirsten sat at his feet on the wicker couch, while Grace sat across the room eyeing him severely. "Are you ready to talk to us?" asked Grace. "You know why we've come, don't

133

you? You know you wanted us to come so that you could tell us the truth."

Louis nodded, not taking his black eyes from Grace. "Yeah, I know. 'Cause I'm the ghost."

Kirsten patted his foot under the blanket. "Tell us why you did all those things."

Louis drank his lemonade to the last drop before he answered. All the time he watched Grace over the rim of his glass. He did not look at Kirsten. Finally he began.

"There was nothin' to do in that place we lived at. Manuel was either sleepin' or workin' all the time. When he had any time at all he was out with some girl or other. An' he picked on me because I read all the time. But I like to read—specially mysteries.

"Then I read a book about how a boy was a poltergeist in an old house—haunted it, you know. And I thought, why not? Why not go to that house where Manuel hung out when he wasn't home or off somewhere?

"Fun, I thought. So I did it all. I planned it a little bit at a time. Like that night you came, Kirsten." For a second he looked at the girl, then away again. "I didn't know about that burglar alarm. I learned that the hard way." He laughed directly into Kirsten's guarded smile.

"You never noticed me around there, Mrs. Douglas. You just knew I was Manuel's little brother, and you always paid a lot of attention to Manuel because he likes history or because he's good-lookin', I don't know which.

"So I stayed hid in a wardrobe in one of those upstairs bedrooms till you closed up for the night. I planned to play some loud music on my transistor about midnight. I thought I'd scare you both sky-high. Only I was tired so I got into bed and went to sleep in that end bedroom next to the porch. I never even knew it was the one Mr. Stevenson used to sleep in.

"I came to all of a sudden an' didn't know where I was. I got panicky an' run through the hall an' opened a closed door and that set off the burglar alarm. Next thing I knew

I heard you all an' the police comin' in downstairs. So I skun into the furnace room. Funny none of you remembered that place has a furnace in it."

"But after we went away, Louis, I set that alarm and it went off again."

"Yeah, an' that's when I figured out how it must work. That time I hid in a broom closet downstairs when the cops come back. Of course they never thought to look in there, it's so small—little narrow space hardly bigger than a broom. Big enough for me, but they were expectin' a man, I guess. Anyway, they never found me either time, an' I was sure tickled fit to kill. I thought I'd have me some fun that way again soon."

"But, Louis, a lot of things were stolen. Surely you knew that was wrong."

He had bit into a cookie. Now he put it down on the couch beside him and looked annoyed. "I didn't take all that stuff, Mrs. Douglas. I heard you talk about it at your desk once. Different people must have stole different things they could hide in their purses or pockets. A lot of silly stuff like soap dishes an' lace doilies. You think a *boy* would take them? An' that crazy old gold thimble on the fancy table upstairs. What would I do with that kind of stuff?"

His frown changed into an engaging smile. "I did take that little Scotch bagpipe off that doll though. I didn't know it was valuable. I just thought it was cute. I don't have many things."

Kirsten nodded, carefully not looking at her aunt. Harry was pretending to be engrossed in the evening paper. "Of course it was wrong, though, to steal it. I'm glad you didn't take the candle snuffer and the kid-glove stretchers and the other things. My aunt always did think some of the visitors were light-fingered. Didn't you, Aunt Grace?"

"Yes, but I didn't expect Louis to steal." Grace was still very severe. "The museum is state property, you know, Louis."

Louis spoke into the pause that followed this solemn declaration. "I'll give back that little Scotch bagpipe and the Spanish clothes. I hid them under my bed when I took 'em one night."

"What about the time the music box played when it was locked and we were right in the room?" said Kirsten. "Did you have anything to do with that?"

Louis grinned. "No. It really was an earthquake that set it off, I guess. I had a lot of other stuff planned, though. I had a book of magic tricks, showed how you could rig up some strings like a cat's cradle an' things would fall down when you just moved a finger."

"I suppose the night we heard the music in the Stevenson bedroom, that was your transistor."

"Sure it was. An' I moved the chairs around too, played ghost all over the room. Skipped under the bed before you come an' looked in." Louis looked roguish, and Kirsten reflected that he still did not realize the seriousness of his behavior.

"I suppose you thought it was funny when you left that note in the Stevenson bedroom, 'I shall return,' or something like that."

" ' Each month I come back in the dark of the moon,' " quoted Louis with a smile. "I wrote that in invisible ink that showed up lavender when the light hit it. Wasn't that neat?"

"No, it was extremely naughty. Did you have some reason for punishing me? Didn't you like me?"

Louis looked stricken. "I like you fine. Did you think someone was mad at you when all those things happened?"

Grace nodded. "And then Mr. Weidman, he's always been good to you, hasn't he? And what did you do? Stole the trunk room key off his key ring."

"But I had to, don't you see? That's when I decided it would be better to sleep down there instead of upstairs in the room you call the Stevenson one. Less chance of bein' found out. Only then you saw me one night."

Kirsten stared at him so intently that he looked first to

136

one side, then to the other, finally at his feet. "Louis, look at me and tell me. Didn't your conscience trouble you when you did all those things?"

He nodded without looking at her. "Just a tiny bit. But it was fun," he insisted. "An' there was nothin' to do at home."

"And when you took that little bagpipe, didn't you know you were taking something that belonged to the whole State of California?"

His eyes looked bigger than usual in his pale face. "Gee, I never thought about that. Just thought I was stealin' from you, Mrs. Douglas."

"Well, even from me! I don't like to have my things taken away. Suppose I stole something of yours?"

Her tone was severe but his answer was gay with assurance. "You wouldn't do that."

"No, I wouldn't, dear." Grace stood up and Kirsten leaned down to hug Louis. "I think we've visited long enough for the first time," her aunt said.

Louis peeped at Grace over Kirsten's shoulder. "You're not really mad at me?"

She dropped beside him and hugged him too. "Of course I'm not mad at you. Just worried. You're too nice not to know the difference between right and wrong."

"Aunt Maria says she'll teach me a lot."

Kirsten brightened. "How very lucky you are, Louis. Well, we're off, honey."

Grace, too, said goodnight, but she did not smile. She was not quite ready to forgive this naughty young ghost.

14

When next Kirsten saw Manuel it was in the garden behind Stevenson House. She came on him as he was looking
thoughtfully at the cobwebby window of the trunk room.
Probably he was thinking of his little brother, of the lone-
liness that had caused Louis to seek out this strange spot.
She surprised a contrite expression in Manuel's eyes.

"Oh, Kirsten, hi. You caught me, didn't you? How could
I have been so blind? My own brother. You have no idea
how dear he is to me."

"Maybe I do, Manuel. You mustn't brood about it. You
did what you thought was right. Now you know you're on
the right track. Everyone agrees that Louis is where he belongs. You just can't fight traffic."

"I sure tried to for a long time."

Soon Manuel was again his sunny self and plans for the
Baile de los Cascarones seemed important to the four young
people.

"Aunt Grace still doesn't know a thing about it," chuckled Kirsten one morning. "She can't understand why I've suddenly become so interested in learning to dance old-fashioned waltzes. She came on me last night after supper, twirling in the living room. I really think she wondered if I had lost my mind."

"Everything is shipshape," responded Jane. The armory is engaged and the California Combo is rarin' to go."

"I only hope my aunt will enjoy this party," said Kirsten doubtfully. "I've put all my energy into it, and so have you. What if it's all wasted?"

That evening Kirsten sat with her aunt in the living room in the agreeable companionship they had learned to share.

"What a honeymoon story!" said the girl, putting down *The Silverado Squatters*. She stretched her arms above her head and relaxed against the back of the comfortable old wing chair. "Do you suppose they were happy, Aunt Grace?"

"Stevenson and Fannie Osbourne? I feel sure from all I've ever read about them that they were happy, Kirsten. Yet it was an unconventional marriage for their time—she was much older than he, and a divorced woman with a sixteen-year-old daughter and two small sons. One of the boys died in Paris when he was only four.

"I think that she sometimes had too much to say about Stevenson's writing. She even suggested changes in his stories sometimes, I believe. But any woman can be forgiven for a little managing, especially if the man is much younger than she. And she was surely what he needed. He was so frail, you know.

"He first came over to this country because he heard that she was near death. In the years that followed she nursed him through many illnesses. They were married in San Francisco the spring after he left this house."

"I've read everything he ever wrote, I guess," said Kirsten proudly. "Some I'd read before and this summer I read that whole row of books on the top shelf in my bedroom. A lot of people might think that was a waste of time. They would say I should have been cross-stitching towels to put in my kitchen when I'm married."

The girl rose from her chair and went to stand over the heater in the floor between the living room and the hall, relishing its warmth on the chilly August evening.

"The fact is, Aunt Grace, I'm not a bit sure I want to get married right away. I suppose the reason both you and my parents wanted me to come out here was so that I'd see some sense."

"I wouldn't put it that way, dear. Your father's words were, 'Give her a chance to get some perspective on her life.' He was afraid you had always been taken for granted as their oldest, a handy baby-sitter for the others. Your mother, who may have seen your problem even more clearly because she's a woman, wrote me that she felt you were being 'untrue to yourself' in your engagement to Roger."

"Did she really? I never thought Mama understood. I thought she always thrust me at boys as if she was afraid I wasn't appealing. And then when one boy wanted to marry me she tried to draw me back against my will."

"Adults are usually strange creatures to young people."

"It hit me all of a sudden. I actually don't want to cross-stitch tea towels and write out recipes, not for a while anyway. I keep thinking of the things I would have missed if I'd settled down in an apartment with Roger—silly things like walking along Fisherman's Wharf, surfing at Pacific Grove, seeing the ocean at Point Lobos."

"You call those silly?"

"I mean they weren't important to me. At least not at first. But now they are. I'm learning to know myself." She spoke hesitantly, smoothing down her pink skirt, which billowed out from the heat of the gas fire. "What are you sewing?" she asked.

Her aunt laughed. "I'm cross-stitching tea towels," she admitted, and Kirsten joined in her laughter.

"I didn't mean to offend you when I implied that it was a waste of time."

"You didn't. After all, I'm forty years old. Time isn't so important to me. And my first tea towels have long ago worn out. I suddenly realized how nice some new ones would be with a little handwork on them."

"Would you like me to make some cocoa?"

"My dear, I don't dare enjoy cocoa with you till I lose a few pounds. Your cookies haven't done my girlish figure any good."

"Bouillon then."

"Fine."

Presently her aunt put down her sewing and they sat at the kitchen table together spooning up the hot amber liquid. Grace said, in the voice of one half fearful of an angry outburst, "You haven't worn your ring for a while, dear."

"No." Kirsten tipped up her cup and drank the last of her bouillon. "I can't make up my mind about Roger."

"Do you want to talk about it?"

"I think so." Kirsten folded her hands. "I was so proud when Roger fell in love with me because I wasn't an ugly duckling any more."

"You certainly were never ugly."

Kirsten flashed her a look of gratitude. "Thanks, Aunt Grace. What I was when Roger began to go with me was a kind of mama's girl. Really a square. When I baby-sat for my folks I felt very virtuous. I said it was so they could have a good time. And Lorna. But really I had a built-in excuse not to try to compete with other girls for dates. I didn't respect myself as a girl.

"I didn't care about my clothes, whether I wore a polka dot blouse with a flowered skirt. When I got a rip in anything I just gathered it up with a safety pin. And I never carried a hankie, just sniffed instead. I told myself I didn't care whether boys asked me out. I didn't mind being left with my brothers and sisters. I was a resigned homebody. That was unforgivable to the kids in high school. Everybody belonged to some gang. All I had was fat Em Glade. Most kids my own age made me freeze up.

"So Roger did a lot for me. He was a nice boy and a good athlete. Not the most popular fellow either, or he wouldn't have singled me out. But he belonged, you know, because he was on the team, and then he drove that little red M.G.

"I didn't mind his getting angry with me sometimes. I thought he had a right to. And he did look handsome when he was in a rage! But now I've decided—well, I just wouldn't take it any more if he criticized me for being 'quaint.' I like being quaint, if that's what I am."

"You've raised your voice a good bit," said her aunt mildly. "You needn't shout at me. I'm glad you've got some spunk."

"It isn't spunk, it's self-respect. Maybe I ought to tell you this. Roger wrote me a few weeks ago that he had taken my sister Lorna out on a date. He was too apologetic, so I suspected that he was feeling guilty. And do you know what happened? I began immediately to daydream that I was out with Harry at times when Roger and Lorna were perhaps going somewhere together.

"I dream of Harry sometimes, and I dreamed of Manuel for a while. I thought I was in love with Manuel. That's when I asked you what you would do if you couldn't decide between two men, and you said wait for a third to come along.

"I think it was the very next morning after you said that that I met Harry. Once I would have believed that I was in love with Harry. Now I won't let myself call any of my feelings love. I'm too young. And I just don't know."

"Kirsten, why don't you turn in the other half of your ticket and stay here with me this winter?"

The girl's blood pounded so that for a moment things seemed to go black and then too bright. She had dreamed of being asked to stay, perhaps to go to Monterey Peninsula College in the winter. Harry would be going there.

But she shook her head. "I have to go back home," she said. "I couldn't write Roger a 'Dear John' letter. I think I'll go to a teacher's college this winter, go home weekends, and sort myself out a little. I've got to do things the way my conscience tells me to. But I do thank you for asking me. And if you want me to come back next summer . . ."

"I'm asking you right now, my dear."

Kirsten gave her aunt a hug, which Grace returned with fervor.

"You know, I didn't want to go to college for the silliest reason—because Roger's grades weren't good enough and he would have resented my being better educated than he. He was always sneering about intellectual women. Imagine!"

"I can easily imagine it. What you have, dear, isn't just brains." She laughed and hurried on, "You have skill with people because you love them."

The days of August ran away like a brook, sparkling and noisy. Jane and Manuel continually argued and then made up, flashing in and out of the steady friendship of Kirsten and Harry like blue jays quarreling in a quiet garden.

The magnolia tree bloomed, one or two big flowers at a time, pointing their pale green buds to the sky, gradually opening for one full day's blossoming, one long night of fragrance. Then the cream-colored burnt-out flowers clung to the tree, dropping an occasional curled petal to the carpet of ivy below.

Kirsten stared into the clustered glossy leaves in the heart of the tree one night after she was in bed. Finally she put on her light and wrote the two letters she knew she must not delay sending. The first was to her parents.

Dear folks,

I feel as though time were running away from me. I have to leave here on September 2, to use the other half of my round-trip fare. Even though I love you all dearly, I don't exactly want to come home. I want to make something of myself before I settle down, and I don't want to marry anyone for a while. I'm writing Roger tonight too. I'd like to go to teacher's college and end up perhaps with a certificate to teach in the grades.

Or perhaps I might major in sociology. I've discovered that I deal well with people. Maybe being the oldest of six helped. Maybe baby-sitting and making cookies for them all was more important than I realized. I do want my own family some day —but not yet, not too soon. Children are too important to start out being resented because they've closed doors to other interests.

Aunt Grace has asked me to come back here next summer and I want to do it.

Your loving daughter,
Kirsten

Without giving herself too much time to think she wrote her other letter:

Dear Roger,

I'll be home some time on September 5. I've been thinking that if you really want to go into the Navy it might be a wise thing to do. I know now that I'm not mature enough in many ways to marry yet. I wouldn't be a good wife nor a good mother for a few years.

I am not saying now that I will never marry you. I cannot marry though till I'm sure of myself.

Sincerely your friend,
Kirsten

Excitement over the coming dance heightened among the four young friends as the month wore on. Kirsten enjoyed the sense of conspiracy that filled her days. Each morning, until her aunt went down to her desk at nine-thirty, Kirsten acted as though she had not a plan in the world other than preparing for her trip back home. On Grace's free days, she agreed to any plan her aunt might suggest for spending their time. They shopped in Carmel for gifts for all the members of Kirsten's family, and visited some of Grace's friends. Kirsten and the friends behaved as though there had been no exchange between them of invitation and acceptance to a wonderful masked ball.

But during the hours when Grace was at work her niece

was geared to action. With Jane she checked over the list of guests and planned the refreshments. "We'd better make it just punch and cookies. Aunt Grace complains I've been fattening her up. No sandwiches."

"Oh, of course not. Though it would be fun to make fancy gelatin shapes and things like that."

"Too complicated." For once Kirsten was not only the practical one, but the one in charge of details. "May we make the cookies at your house, Jane? Aunt Grace can smell fresh cookies a mile away."

"Of course. Mama will be glad to have us around. She really took to you."

"Then let's gather up all the empty coffee cans we can lay our hands on and go to work. You call Manuel's aunt, and if she has any he can bring them in when he comes to work. I'll tackle Harry. Perhaps the supermarket has some empty coffee cans in the warehouse."

In the days that followed they made enough cookies to feed not just seventy but seven times seventy people. "We must surely have enough," said Kirsten. "That's seven kinds we've done now. Isn't it fun?"

"Manuel asked me last night if his Aunt Maria could make the punch," said Jane. "She wants to help in some way. She's so grateful to your aunt for getting Louis out of trouble."

"Gee, maybe we should have invited Maria and Pedro to the party."

"Oh, they wouldn't expect that. They aren't really friends of your aunt's. But they do beautiful specialty dances for parties sometimes."

Kirsten's eyes shone. "That's an idea!" Then she turned back to her list of duties and checked off "cookies and punch." Harry's mother had promised them her punch bowl and a long lace tablecloth. "Now we have to go to the armory and arrange for extra punch glasses and see about janitor services."

"And don't forget, you have to get something for the people in the dance combo."

Kirsten looked faintly embarrassed. "I don't have the least notion how many people are in a combo," she admitted.

"Well, in this one there's the pianist, and besides her there's a trombone, a sax, a trumpet, and the drums. They're marv, and I know them all. The trombonist is a friend of Dad's. The sax and trumpet players are two brothers who run a shoe store on Alvarado, and the boy on drums was just a year ahead of me in high school."

"Well, let's go to the armory first."

The building was just a few blocks away, and when they arrived Jane cried, "Why, we can kill two birds with one stone. This is the day the Soroptimists are having their big rummage sale."

First they found the janitor in his office and after they had arranged for the extra glasses, Kirsten asked hesitantly, "About your charges . . ."

"Five dollars would take care of everything," said the janitor. "Mrs. Douglas is a favorite of mine. I worked at Stevenson House for a little while. I'd do it for nothing," he smiled in some embarrassment, "but then my wife would say, 'Where you been all evening?' "

Kirsten thanked him, and then followed Jane into the hall of the armory. She was amused by Jane's delight. She moved among the heaped tables of the rummage sale as eagerly as though she were being offered all the beauties of the Orient and the perfumes of Arabia.

"Why, it's mostly junk," whispered Kirsten in disgust.

"You don't know, Kirstie," answered Jane. "You have to learn how to look. How do you ever expect to keep house if you don't know how to find bargains. There!" She swooped down on a table of old dishes and kitchen utensils.

Unerringly she reached for a small fluted bowl edged in gold. On its inner surface were painted several creamy small roses and faded green leaves. Expertly Jane turned it over and pointed triumphantly to the words stamped on the bottom: "Haviland Limoges." The price written in the bowl in black crayon was thirty-five cents.

She held it out to the woman behind the table who was busy wrapping an ancient waffle iron. When Kirsten had paid for the bowl and received it back in a paper bag, Jane chortled, "That's a find, Kirstie. Mrs. Gould is absolutely crazy about Haviland. If you'd found that in an antique shop it would probably have cost three dollars. Now what else?"

Kirsten had spotted a table of books away at the back of the hall. Here was one place where her knowledge would serve better than Jane's. "Look, Jane, do you suppose any of those books are in good condition? I can always find a book that will suit as a gift."

"Some of them will be like new." Jane laughed. "You don't know how many people have books on their shelves for years without cracking 'em. Come on."

It turned out that Jane was better after all at picking out the proper books because she knew the interests of the musicians. They chose an excellent illustrated garden book on bonsai for the trombonist, the untouched works of Jane Austen (in a cheap edition) for the shoe-store brothers, and Whitman's *Leaves of Grass* for the drummer, who had secret poetic yearnings. Kirsten received change from a five dollar bill. "What a morning!" she chuckled.

"Let's get back and wrap them before your aunt gets up to the apartment for lunch. Then I'll sneak them down the back stairs and into Dad's pickup. We'll keep them at my house till the night of the party. Oh, Kirstie, isn't this fun?"

15

With the dawn of August 30, the day of the dance, Kirsten realized that the things one looks forward to most joyfully can sometimes be the saddest. Her days were shadowed now with the knowledge of her leaving. There were moments when she wished Roger and she had never made plans for a future together.

And yet if she had not thought she was in love with him her parents would not have sent her out here for the summer. And she would not have met Manuel and Jane and Harry. Perhaps she would not have become acquainted with herself until it was too late.

Jane still wore Manuel's signet ring around her neck. When she was safely away from her parents she put it on the third finger of her left hand and kept the hand in Manuel's, squeezing it possessively when she saw him looking at any other pretty girl. Among all her other activities of the past weeks she had finished the Empress Eugénie costume in apricot satin. The long dress had a high waistline and she had made a hat in matching color with one swept-up brim and a mass of curled ostrich plumes cascading down the other side.

Kirsten envied Jane this sewing skill. She herself had finally decided to wear her old senior prom dress. Her mother had made it, and Kirsten was glad she had decided to bring it with her. "I'll go as a sweet girl graduate," she said, laughing, as she tried it on for Jane that morning. "I told Aunt Grace Harry had asked me to a dance at the armory tonight, but I just couldn't tell her it's a costume affair. She'd try to find out more about it if it seemed like a big deal. Mr. Weidman got the velvet trousseau gown from the Custom House. His wife will bring it along with a mask for Aunt Grace to wear. She can dress in the powder room. Harry's going to ask her to go along with us to see the special decorations. Then he promised to bring her right home again. Oh, Jane, I'm dying of excitement. I've never before surprised anyone, really."

After supper Kirsten bathed and dressed for the ball. When she came out into the living room, holding a white satin mask in her hand, her aunt turned her around and said quietly, "You're lovely, Kirsten, truly lovely."

The green velvet bodice fitted her figure snugly, and the white skirt flared out and floated around her. Her short dark hair was shining and the touch of green eye shadow on her lids made her dark eyes look enormous.

"Oh, my dear," said Grace. They hugged each other. They were thinking, not of the dance, but of the separation. They heard Harry running up the stairs.

He pushed open the door, holding a square florist's box. Then he saw Kirsten. He came in and walked all around her, holding out the box. His eyes were shining as she opened it and lifted out a spray of pink carnations. But all he said was, "I guess this is our last date, isn't it?"

Kirsten's heart ached. For some reason at this moment she

remembered an admonition of her mother's, "Girls are usually about two years ahead of boys emotionally, but they seldom catch up mentally." Strange to remember her mother's wisdom after all this time of trying to go her own way!

"I won a prize in the fishing derby today," said Harry. "I won second prize for the second biggest salmon of the season. Oh, Kirstie, it was great! It was only a bit over eighteen pounds, but a beauty!"

"What was the prize, Harry?"

"A deep freeze. Of course I'm giving it to my mother. Boy, is she ever excited!"

Aunt Grace added her congratulations and presently Harry was quiet. He moved close to Kirsten as she pinned the corsage on her shoulder.

"You smell good," he said, then turned innocently toward Grace. "You are coming, aren't you, Mrs. Douglas? We want you to see the decorations in the armory."

Grace put her hand to her head. "I have a little headache," she said. "Would you mind coming back for me about nine-thirty? That will give me a chance to take an aspirin and lie down for a while. I do want to see you young people dancing. I haven't been to a dance in donkey's years."

She left them and going into her room closed the door.

"Do you think she suspects?" whispered Kirsten.

"No, I think she's telling the truth. Your aunt always does. Come on, I'll pick her up at nine-thirty. It will be all the better when everyone is there to shout 'Surprise' as she walks in."

They ran down the steps and through the garden to Harry's car. "I've got my mask and a cowboy suit in the trunk," said Harry. "Didn't want to arouse your aunt's suspicions. I'll put them on in the men's room after I've brought her to the dance."

The cars were already lining the streets around the armory and rapidly filling the reserved parking space. Through the windows they could see the large paper-covered chandelier revolving slowly, flashing spots of colored light, like handfuls of jewels, on the dancers.

Suddenly beside Kirsten appeared a pretty blond Empress Eugénie. She had piled her hair high under the hat of curled ostrich plumes, and on one cheek she had pasted a beauty mark. She held tightly the hand of a red devil. Kirsten would have known Manuel anywhere by his short stocky figure and his unruly thick black hair.

"Hi," said Jane happily. "Come on. Everyone's here!"

As they followed Jane and Manuel across the floor, Kirsten shook her head sadly. Everything had changed since they had first planned the dance. She couldn't help thinking of tomorrow, and the day after, and the bus ride back to Ohio.

With pride Jane took her from one couple to another performing the introductions. "It doesn't mean much when everyone is masked," she laughed. "We'll have to introduce you all over again. Guess who this is." Jane laid her hand possessively on a tall man in a green ranger suit and mask.

"The Green Giant," guessed Harry.

But Kirsten grasped his hand and said gladly, "Mr. Tinsley, I'm so glad you came."

"Do you suppose your aunt will let me squire her for the evening?" he asked. "I think I might even manage a waltz if she's willing."

"I'm sure she will be."

"Time to get her," said Harry and he left the hall.

For a moment Kirsten felt a return of her old shyness. But this was no time to panic. She went to the piano and played a few loud chords to get attention. Then she called out, "Everyone stand around the edges of the room. We'll turn the lights out in a minute and stay in the dark till we hear Harry and my aunt coming up the walk. Then as they step in, the lights will go on. And please all yell 'Surprise' as loud as you can."

And so it happened. If Grace had still had her headache the noise of the shouting would have caused her acute distress. But as the lights came on and she saw all her friends, holding their masks now so that she would know who they were, her face broke into a radiant smile.

"Oh, Kirsten, darling, what a lovely thing for you to do." She knew at once who had planned it all.

Mr. Tinsley bowed before her. "May I have the pleasure of this dance?" he asked with mock formality. "They've promised it is to be a waltz."

"But not before we dress her in her costume," said Jane. "Come on, Mrs. Douglas." The long dress of embroidered dark-red velvet fit her perfectly and she returned to the hall to walk proudly among her friends. And so the dance began.

The hours flew and Kirsten was aware each time her eyes sought out her aunt that the idea had been a good one and the evening was a success. It was eleven o'clock before she knew it. At a signal the dancers stopped and moved to the sides of the big room. The orchestra fell silent and the lack of noise was more exciting than the ear-splitting music had been. Four guitarists stepped out from another room and a pair of masked dancers moved onto the cleared dance floor. The couple wore the Spanish costumes Kirsten had seen in the trunk room. The woman was as slim and dark as the man, though neither was very tall. Kirsten recognized Pedro Castro's high cheekbones and thin, sleek head. There was subtle grace in all his movements. And his partner of course was Aunt Maria.

The music became wildly exciting and the crowd stamped its feet and clapped its hands.

"Cocoroco," Manuel crowed along with the musicians, imitating the sound of a cock. Kirsten had never seen Manuel so happy before. Catching her eye, he smiled and blew her a kiss.

The dancers never lost step, never missed a beat as they changed to a Chilean *Cueca*. While Maria snapped the castanets above her head, Pedro beat out the rhythm on the floor with his silver spurs. The watchers kept a fascinated silence. The courting dance ended with Pedro kneeling before Maria, who tonight looked young and beautiful.

Kirsten turned a questioning glance toward Manuel. "I asked them if they would come and dance for us," he said. "They do these dances at their sodality parties. Max got the costumes back from your aunt."

Kirsten did not have a chance to ask about Louis, for just then a small hand grasped hers and a small happy voice said, "Pretty good, eh, Kirstie?"

"Very good," said Kirsten, and stooping, hugged the boy.

But the music of the encore had ended and he pulled away, saying proudly, "I gotta go back or Mama will worry. We're going home after this dance."

Pedro and Maria came up to Kirsten and her aunt with outstretched hands. "But you can't go until after the *Baile de los Cascarones*," Kirsten whispered so that her aunt could not hear. "Please stay."

The music started again and the orchestra played "The Spanish Cavalier." Kirsten remembered the time the music box in Stevenson House had played the song. Softly she sang:

> "Oh, say, darling, say,
> When I'm far away
>   Sometime you may think of me, dear.
> Bright, sunny days
> Will soon fade away.
>   Remember what I say and be true, dear."

She realized that Harry did not feel the same way she did about their parting, but she did not feel guilty that three months ago she would have sung this song to Roger. He would probably have said, even though moved by the words and her husky voice, "Don't be quaint, Kid."

Now señoritas with large baskets full of beautifully decorated eggs—blue and green and yellow, dark red, wood-brown, and gold—moved through the crowd.

153

Kirsten's eyes were on her aunt's face and she was happy at the look Grace gave her.

"Oh, Kirsten, *cascarones*. How wonderful! Where did you ever get so many?"

"We made them," Kirsten said proudly. "Jane and I made them at her house."

Manuel chose a pale-green egg for Jane on which Jane herself had painted a seascape with one white curling blue-green wave.

Harry let the basket go by and when Kirsten turned her dark eyes on him, he took a tissue-wrapped egg from the pocket of his cowboy shirt. It was painted a delicate pink and had a gold crescent moon pasted over either end.

Harry held the *cascarón* above Kirsten's head.

"Don't," she cried. "I want to save it."

"Oh no, my dear, I didn't get this egg for you to save forever!" Harry crushed the shell, and a shower of gold— real gold dust—fell down over Kirsten's soft dark hair. There were gasps and cries of delight around them, then a profusion of broken *cascarones* and bright confetti all over the hall.

Harry swept Kirsten into his arms and began to dance down the golden space before they were thickly surrounded by other dancers. Jane's voice followed them. "Kirsten, *real gold dust!* You must be very proud."

But Kirsten was remembering not gold dust at all, but the words, "my dear." She leaned her head against Harry's shoulder and her steps perfectly followed his, even as she thought dreamily, "Whoever said Harry wasn't a good dancer?"

It was Kirsten's last night in Monterey. The *Baile de los Cascarones* was a memory. Her bus would leave the next morning at eight.

She had spent the day walking through Stevenson House and had stopped for a smiling farewell before the dark oil portrait of R.L.S.

She had said goodbye to the gardener and the janitor and even the policemen, and had wandered one last time from one end of the garden to the other. That evening Harry asked her to go to a movie, but she shook her head.

"I'd rather just go for a walk."

They walked the streets until they saw on a drugstore clock that it was midnight. Then they went slowly back to Stevenson House and sat on the bench beneath the magnolia tree.

Harry reached for Kirsten's hand. "This is what I will remember this winter," he said. "Will you remember too?"

"Yes."

He opened her hand and spread her fingers, looking down at them in the half dark. "You are going to write to me?"

She spoke with difficulty. "You know I will."

"Do you think you'll come back next year?" he asked after a silence. "If only you didn't have to leave, we could go steady just as friends for a few years."

"Could we, Harry?"

"I don't know. But this way, with you leaving, it makes it too serious too soon." He pulled her to her feet. "The more you care," he said in a troubled voice, "the less you can show it. I wonder why people always say youth is such a wonderful time of life. Sometimes it's nothing but waiting."

Grace woke Kirsten at six. They had their usual breakfast and this time it was Kirsten who mentioned the vicar's egg.

"I'll always remember that, Aunt Grace. 'Parts of it, my lord, were excellent.'"

"I guess that was the way with your summer," said her aunt, pouring coffee. "Parts of it were excellent."

"All of it, Aunt Grace—all of it."

"Are you packed?"

"All ready."

Kirsten went to her room for her purse and suitcase. Her aunt followed her. "It's not too late, Kirsten, to change your mind. Your parents have five children left, and it would be good for Lorna to be in charge of the younger ones for a while. How about it?"

Kirsten's heart began sliding this way and that, like a

skidding car on a wet pavement. "What do you mean—not too late?"

"You could wire your folks and get a refund on your bus ticket." Her aunt's voice was tight with excitement.

But Kirsten knew her own mind now. "No, Aunt Grace," she said gently, throwing her arms around her aunt's neck. "No, I must go home."

A little after seven, Kirsten opened the door to Harry and Jane. Jane carried an armful of magazines and Harry a box of candy.

"I'm going to miss you, Kirstie," Jane cried in a gush of pleasurable sentiment.

Harry said nothing as they went out. Kirsten stood on the porch a moment looking across to the door of the Stevenson bedroom. Beyond the garden came faintly the noises of Monterey awakening.

"Too bad this house doesn't have a view," said Harry, making conversation.

"A *view*!" Kirsten was surprised. "Why, I've seen everything from here, Harry. My whole life and everyone in it."

As they went down the stairs into the brick-paved patio, the morning fog shrouded the garden. Only the heavier, darker trees and shrubs stood out of the milky moisture, black on gray.

Kirsten would have sworn she saw a ghostly figure, tall and thin, with a narrow skull and slender feet and a rather tattered coat, whisk around a corner of the building and disappear into the mist.

It was the last she ever saw of the ghost of Stevenson House.

ABOUT THE AUTHOR

ALBERTA ARMER published her first children's book in 1958. Since that time she has gained a reputation as a distinguished children's book author. Among her most recent books are *Troublemaker, Steve and the Guide Dogs,* and *Screwball.* Born in Indiana and raised in Michigan, Mrs. Armer was graduated from the University of California at Berkeley and has been variously a magazine writer, an editor, and a teacher. The mother of three children, and a grandmother, she lives with her husband in Davis, California.